REPRISE

REPRISE

Leslie Stephan

ST. MARTIN'S PRESS
NEW YORK

Design by Glen M. Edelstein

Library of Congress Cataloging-in-Publication Data

Stephan, Leslie.
    Reprise.

    "A Thomas Dunne book."
    I. Title.
PS3569.T3827R4   1988   813'.54   88-15835
ISBN 0-312-02272-7

First Edition

10 9 8 7 6 5 4 3 2 1

REPRISE

CHAPTER 1

"Now, now," MYRON STREETER broke in hastily, in his role as chairman of the Hampford Tricentennial Pageant Committee, "acrimony is not on the agenda."

A group of seven, the committee was meeting this April evening in the Board of Assessors' office in the town hall, crowded around a rectangular table that ordinarily held surveyors' maps. Chosen to represent all potentially supportive segments of the population, they also represented seven divergent points of view, and Myron was wishing fervently that he knew a few more synonyms for *compromise*.

For Sergeant David Putnam, tonight was a first exposure to cooperative creativity. Hampford's chief of police, Leonard Henderson, had left earlier that morning for Virginia to attend the wedding of his niece Agnes, in whose simple ceremony all three of his own daughters were taking part. The cousins were good, dull, cheerful young women, still referred to within the family as "girls," although Agnes and Len's Mary must be pushing thirty-five. The little outing was the high point of their year.

Chief Henderson, who was pathologically anxious about leaving authority in the hands of Sergeant Putnam, had been torn by indecision for a week, but the concerted will of his womenfolk had finally worn him down. He was salving his conscience with the intention of routing his return trip through New Haven, Connecticut, where a conference of southern New England law enforcement officials would consider the issue of juvenile offenders. Hampford's juveniles offended at the level of stealing mailboxes and ripping up street signs, but Chief Henderson felt that, with the world in its current mess, foresight spelled survival, and he fully expected to arm himself with a number of helpful strategies—that is, if Sergeant Putnam did not let the department go straight to hell in his absence.

On the contrary, Sergeant Putnam, in his diligence to fill his chief's shoes, had dutifully taken his seat at the Board of Assessors' table, where he was now feeling both sleepy and superfluous. Len had been a natural choice for the committee, being for many years involved with the Historical Society, as well as a lifelong resident of Hampford with a fund of anecdotal recollections. Surely, that, too, was Bea Lambert's function, since Bea, who was in her seventies, was a repository of local lore. Myron, as chairman of the board of selectmen and president of Homestead Furniture, had the executive experience necessary to manage such a disparate group. Laurel Bradford was a young newcomer, very active in the Bristol Footlighters, with whom she had appeared last winter in a rousing production of *Yentl*. Scott Coffin, coach and history teacher at the high school, had been selected to entice the youth of the town into participation, and Merlin Stroud was quite frankly a minority representative, a result of the effort to touch all bases—in this case the remnant of the Wompanaki Indians who inhabited an area of West Hampford known locally as "Dogtown."

Last but not least, Orianna Soule, as the town's only published author, was a natural choice for any literary undertaking. With bangles jangling on her wrists and hot-pink plastic hoops dangling from her earlobes, Orianna's appearance was "arty" enough to convince Hampford's more provincial citizens of her superior qualifications—an assessment with which Orianna fully concurred.

The meeting had started quite amicably. The pageant committee had previously agreed on a format of five or six scenes, arranged chronologically, from different periods in the town's past and had requested that Orianna bring to the meeting rough notes for the first two or three of these scenes. Orianna shuffled her sheets of yellow lined paper and allowed her fellow citizens a glimpse into the creative process.

"My first thought," she'd told them, "was of those intrepid adventurers who explored and mapped this area. Some of you may be familiar with Maudlin Winesop's journal and his description of 'ye lions and ye unicorns roaring in the forests of thornie brambel.' He

3

mistook a skunk for a white rabbit, poor fellow, and paid a heavy price for his ignorance. However, despite its fascination, I found the period too limiting. Better, it seemed to me, would be a village scene involving large colorful groups, and what more appropriate groups than Indians and settlers—buckskin and linsey-woolsey, as it were."

"Burlap makes a super substitute for buckskin," Laurel Bradford put in eagerly.

"With masses of beads."

Exactly! Eyes shining, the two women contemplated a vision that eluded the rest of the gathering.

"Just what are these two groups going to *do?*" asked Myron on behalf of the less imaginative.

"Oh, I have the scene all mapped out. I've been up to my ears in town records and *A History of Wessex County*. Here we are. I'm focusing on a single day before the Bloody Shambles Massacre of 1686."

"We call it 'The Day of Shame,'" said Merlin Stroud.

"Well, whatever," Orianna replied airily. "The thing is Hampford in 1686 was surrounded by marauding savages who did not recognize the legality of a King's Grant."

"Legality," snorted Merlin. "How can it be legal to give away land that's not yours to give?"

"So forget about legal. We're interested in drama. Just listen to this. There was a Wompanaki Indian named Joseph Handy."

"His name was Metachumpamixalot," said Merlin. "It means Born-With-No-Brains."

"The settlers called him Joseph."

"They should have called him Uncle Tom."

4

"Now, listen, Merlin, for the sake of getting out of here sometime tonight, why don't you let Orianna tell her story and then we'll discuss it," Myron said diplomatically.

"Thank you, Myron. This Joseph was a kind of prime minister or something."

Merlin snorted again but held his tongue.

"In any case, he spoke English. And one day he came to Hampford and he said, Listen here, you're having trouble with the Bagawumps and so are we. We'll stop harassing you if you'll give us muskets to fight against the Bagawumps. So off they marched, whooping and hollering, and the Bagawumps wiped them out."

"I thought you said they had muskets," Scott Coffin put in.

"What good are muskets," Merlin explained bitterly, "when there are four hundred Bagawumps and twenty-eight Wompanakis. Joseph Handy was the dumbest Indian who ever walked the face of the earth."

"That's not the point," Orianna said impatiently. "Our scene takes place *before* the massacre, which nobody, frankly, has to know about. The settlers and the Indians held a sort of ceremony to cement the pact, with a roasted ox and a whole day of feasting and visiting and general goodwill, and that's what I'd like to portray. Here," she said, selecting a sheet of paper. "This will give you the flavor:

"PELETIAH BIRDLIME: (*Placing beaver hat on J. Handy's head.*) May this cone of ye skin of ye beaver be to ye a symbol of ye everlasting, undying friendship between ourselves and ye sons of the forest.

JOSEPH HANDY: (*On behalf of the Wompanaki tribe,*

5

whose members nod and smirk.) Oh, powerful and esteemed pale man from distant places, we wish with all our hearts to do your bidding. Kill the Bagawumps! (*Chorus of bystanders takes up the cry.*) Kill the Bagawumps!

REVEREND ONESIMUS HAGGARD: Go in ye name of God Almighty to rout out these serpents with rattils in their tails, these Devils seeking to devour God's children, these—"

"Stop, I can't take this," Merlin cried. "You've got to be kidding."

"What's the matter now?"

"The matter? It's all hogwash, that's the matter."

"Maybe you could do better?"

"You bet I could."

"Why don't you try, then," said Myron wearily, "and bring us your version next week, and Orianna, you hold on to yours and we'll try to work out a compromise. Now, what was our next scene going to be?"

Whew, thought Sergeant Putnam. Was this how committees worked? Or was it Orianna who was setting off sparks? After three years in Hampford, she remained an enigma, exotic enough to both attract and repel. Raw from a particularly nasty divorce, she had purged her bitterness with her typewriter and the resulting novel, the story of a repressed housewife turned bullfighter, had ridden the crest of the women's movement to great success with its underlying message of male despicability. Not surprisingly, her "brilliant" debut as a "major new talent" had restored her shattered self-confidence, had, indeed, inflated her self-image to heady proportions.

6

On a practical level, the sales of the book had enabled her to buy one of the choicest old Colonial homes in Hampford, which she had proceeded to "renovate" with terrace, skylights, pool, and tennis court, and in which she maintained a life-style both highly visible and lavishly shared. But what of the preceding years? Orianna had contributed enough sly allusions to allow the community to piece together a background of solid middle-class values, some kind of vaguely executive position, and marriage to a gifted, if egotistical and cruel, architect. There was a toughness in Orianna, however, a tenacity of mind and resolve, that caused Sergeant Putnam to suspect this admirable fairy tale, for it was a toughness compatible with a hard scrabble upward from lowly origins. His suspicion was periodically reinforced by forms of grammatical usage not encountered in Hampford's better circles.

Two hours of concourse on top of a full day's work proved frankly soporific, and the sergeant breathed an inward sigh of relief when Myron finally declared the meeting adjourned. Bea Lambert was deep in conversation with Laurel Bradford, so that he was able to slip downstairs without slighting her, which, God forbid, he should ever do, Bea having been, wittingly and unwittingly, a continual source of information to the Hampford Police Department in the past.

The station, on the first floor, lay deep in gloom, barely illuminated by a single desk lamp, which meant Ted Deegan was duty officer. He winced visibly when Sergeant Putnam turned on the overhead fluorescent strips, one of which began a frantic, afflicted winking. Ted's penurious idiosyncracies, annoying as they might be, were more than offset by his dogged application and penchant for tidiness. Law and order was taken literally by Ted to mean just that: a neat police station.

Sergeant Putnam made a quick inspection of the logbook, which in typical Hampford fashion showed one call in two hours. Ted, having already inscribed the entry in his elemental handwriting, was whiling away his shift with a square of needlepoint. The Deegans were collaborating on a set of flowered chair pads.

"Going at it a little hot and heavy, weren't you, Dave? I could hear you way down here," he said.

"Merlin got a bit perturbed."

"Lucky he didn't scalp you, ha-ha."

Such was the level of Ted's humor. He was so amused by his own wit that he had to wipe his eyes. Sergeant Putnam, in disgust, pulled shut the door and clattered down the stairs. It was all well and good for Ted to laugh, but the sergeant was less inclined to dismiss the evening's exchange as comedy. Stirring up rancor was alien to his policeman's instincts.

The fresh April evening, however, quickly dispelled his misgivings, and by the time he had crossed the common, feet crunching on the gravel path, and made his way from one pool of light to the next up Summer Street and on to Cedar Avenue, his perspective had revived.

Davey's bedroom light blazed in solitary brilliance from the dark second floor where the younger children lay asleep. Barbara, ensconced on the living room couch, looked up from her book as he entered. The house was a turn-of-the-century model with all the embellishments of its time, right down to a stained-glass window in the stairwell. Sergeant Putnam took great pride in keeping their period piece in good repair,

8

a dedication that Barbara shared, despite the demands of her job as a teacher's aide at the local elementary school.

"You want a cup of tea?" she asked, stretching lazily.

"I think I'll have a beer."

"How was it?"

"Tiring. Orianna came up with some awful crap about the Indians and Merlin got all uptight. Then we moved on to the Revolutionary War, and damned if she wasn't planning on using the Pulman incident."

"Oh, no." Barbara laughed. "And the Pulmans so proud."

"That's exactly what Bea pointed out. Of course, he wasn't the only Tory in town, but he did get the worst of it, what with that tar and feathering. We tried to explain to Orianna that the Pulmans are still hopping mad, but she regards all these events as ancient history."

"You can't expect an outsider to understand how very much alive they still are."

"They've hardly been defused at all, as we soon found out. I'm referring to the schism in the Congregational Church, around 1840, when twenty families withdrew to become the Orthodox something or other."

"The Orthodox Evangelical Society of Hampford."

"And I suppose it *was* a very colorful period, with the Great Debate and all, but then . . . "

"Then there was that awful ax murder," Barbara said with a shudder. "The Sparhawks have always maintained that Reuben's mind was turned by the rantings of the Orthodox preacher, since he shouted 'Take that, you son of Satan' when he struck, and everyone knew that Ezra Tarbell was a sneering atheist. Why, there

9

are Sparhawks and Tarbells that still don't give each other a good morning. But what about the Civil War?"

"The Women's Relief Corps," Sergeant Putnam said simply.

Barbara responded with an incredulous grin. "Oh, Dave, she didn't."

"What she had in mind, of course, was a scene of the Corps doing a Sunday service at one of the camps, which would have given her a lot of scope, you have to admit, what with soldiers and civilians and a chorus belting out patriotic songs. How was she to know, poor thing, that Women's Relief brought a different kind of relief once it was reorganized by Sergeant Pondexter Viles, that enterprising son of Hampford. The Civil War is a touchy subject, anyway, because of all those deserters."

"Wasn't there a Streeter who hid in a pigpen for a record number of days?"

"Maybe that's why Myron dismissed us rather abruptly. I'm beginning to think Ted is right. We ought to stick to baked bean suppers."

His good mood restored, he locked the back door, shut off the kitchen light, and followed Barbara upstairs.

CHAPTER 2

THE FOLLOWING MORNING, HOWEVER, brought renewed cause for concern, delivered in the person of Bea Lambert, who, with Chief Henderson away, regarded the police station as holding a perpetual open house. Not that she often interrupted anything of significance. On this particular raw spring morning, Sergeant Putnam was perusing a firearms catalog and Everett Hewitt, the fourth and junior member of the department, was draped across the counter, trimming his fingernails with a hunting knife, one of his few concessions to personal hygiene. In fact, Everett was kept as much as possible in the background because of his thoroughly unprofessional appearance. A dirty policeman with third-grade reading skills does not inspire confidence in the general populace. The truth was, Everett's major contribution to the department lay in an area that was never mentioned aloud for fear of ridicule: his psychic powers, a faculty that his superiors were not above tapping as a covert source of enlightenment.

Bea shook herself like a wet dog at the doorway, distributing a sprinkle of raindrops from her transparent pink cape, which she then draped across the back of a plastic chrome-legged chair whose bucket seat, in color and conformation, appeared to simulate a large set of buttocks.

The room was shaped like a coffin. Desks and file cabinets behind the counter marked that section as the domain of the professional staff, while the space in front, with its motley collection of listing plastic chairs, was clearly the province of the general public.

"My goodness, if I hadn't seen a daffodil, I'd have thought it was December," Bea said, fluffing her springy gray curls.

She addressed this remark past Everett, whom she usually, skillfully, managed not to see, but Everett remained cheerfully oblivious to her censure. He did, however, have the grace to close his knife, and after some prodding from Sergeant Putnam shambled into Chief Henderson's office to straighten out the bookcase, whose condition proved definitively that a large amount crammed into a small space will end up on the rug. Out of sight did not necessarily mean out of hearing, since Everett was in the habit of leaving doors ajar; he was, in fact, as inveterate a collector of information as was Bea. The two, had they joined forces, would have made a formidable team, but such a union was forever precluded by Bea's fastidiousness.

Bea, who this week had cast aside all inhibitions, came right around the counter and took a seat beside Sergeant Putnam's desk, from which vantage point her bright eyes soon absorbed and cataloged the miscellaneous papers that lay spread across its surface.

She was dressed in a seasonal amalgam of cotton "wash dress" beneath a snugly buttoned, hand-knit cardigan in her own unique design and favorite shade of pink. Wrinkled lisle stockings covered her thin legs and goodness knows how many layers of warm wool dwelt beneath the brave cotton. She had for years, in the face of inclement weather, made use of a pair of brand-new overshoes unexpectedly left behind by Dear Father, but these, of course, now reposed neatly side by side on the doormat. Bea and Ted Deegan, as members of Hampford's elder generation, were among the final recipients of a set of values that had spanned generations intact. Unaware of the importance of self-fulfillment or the necessity of doing one's own thing, they struggled diligently to mind the childhood admonitions of their parents and teachers to be honest, thrifty, useful, and kind. One did one's duty, convenient or not, and one left one's overshoes at the door.

So there sat Bea, perched on the edge of her chair with her stockings bagging around her ankles, clutching her worn black purse in swollen-knuckled hands, her eyes shining with the anticipation of imparting a bit of gossip that Sergeant Putnam appeared not to have heard.

It seemed that Scott Coffin had driven Orianna to and from the town hall the previous evening, Orianna's car being entombed for a brake job in Chick's Garage in Mount Pleasant. On the way home from the meeting, Orianna, according to Bea, had been "spitting fire." Sergeant Putnam did not attempt to identify the source of her information, knowing from experience that the chain of transmission would eventually come clear. Bea had little tolerance for digression once she was launched into one of her narratives.

"She was pretty cross when we broke up," he agreed.

"She was *furious*," Bea amended. "She had a lot to say about working with amateurs, particularly provincial amateurs who, she said, wouldn't recognize a winner if it hit them on the nose. There was quite a bit along those lines. If we preferred some Tom, Dick, or Harry to herself—she meant poor Merlin—then good luck to us, but one thing we'd better realise, she hadn't done all that research for nothing. If she couldn't use her scenes in the pageant, then she would use them in a book.

"'What kind of book,' Scott asked her, for her statement almost sounded to him like a threat. 'A best-seller,' she told him. Of course, she intended to change the names to protect the innocent."

"Hmmmmm."

"Now, it's my conviction, David, and not mine alone I might add, that the invitation from the pageant committee proved very opportune for Orianna. It's been three years since *Olé* was published, and she has yet to produce a sequel. The truth is, I think she wrote that book in a state of heightened emotion, and without that emotion, she hasn't the ability to write a shopping list. Suddenly and providentially, she has at hand material that just might compensate for her lack of talent. Do

14

you think she's going to have qualms about using it now that she's gotten her feelings hurt? Do you really think she's going to hesitate for a moment because some of those disclosures might be hurtful? Certainly not. She's got a vindictive streak, you know. I've noticed it in little things. It makes you wonder if that architect of hers was quite as sadistic as we've been led to believe."

"Well, yes, I agree, we've heard only Orianna's side of it. But would you really interpret her words as a threat?"

"She might not have meant it that way, or even seen it as such. But it certainly is having the effect of one. Scott recounted the conversation to his parents when he got home, and his father went out and got drunk. Now, I've been cudgeling my brains for some scandal in the Coffin family, and I simply can't come up with anything worse than Minnie bearing Arthur five months after the wedding."

"Do you actually mean to tell me that some juicy tidbit has escaped your eagle eye and twitching nose, Bea?"

"Apparently it has," she answered meditatively. The thought had given her pause. "Which is not to say," she added, flashing a roguish smile, "that I shan't soon track it down.

"However, the point is, David, that if Gil Coffin has something to hide, so do a lot of other people. Orianna is going to make things very hot for herself if she persists with this foolish notion. Why, Lucille Henfield said to me this morning—she's right next door to the Coffins, you know; Wilma Coffin was hanging out her wash when Lucille went to empty her trash and that's how the subject came up, anyway, she said to me—I was in Randall's picking up some yeast, I'm making one of my cherry coffee cakes to take to old Edgar Hallowell this afternoon; he's been off his feed since that operation, can't seem to keep down anything but hot coffee cake—in any case, Lucille said she thinks that we've treated Orianna in a very neighborly way since she moved to town, and Orianna ought to be ashamed of herself, repaying our kindness with a slap in the face."

"She says one dirty thing about me, I'll sue her for a million," Everett said cheerfully from the doorway of Chief Henderson's office, where he unabashedly had been eavesdropping. "My brother Perley, when he got hit by that car, Ma and the old man collected ten grand."

"Seems like it almost pays to get hit every year," Sergeant Putnam commented dryly. "The truth is," he continued, returning to the subject at hand, "Orianna's got a right to use anything she wants in a book as long as she disguises the identities of the people in it. It's not the legal aspect that concerns me, but the moral one."

"Seriously, you're right," Everett agreed. "I got a bad feelin' about Orianna, black-like."

"Probably the aura of her vile temper," Sergeant Putnam said with a laugh, but, as so often happened, Everett's narrow-eyed pronouncement gave him, on a primal level, a prickle of apprehension.

"She's a misguided young woman," Bea summarized tartly, "who might find herself in a peck of trouble."

CHAPTER
3

WITH BEA HEADING BACK to her coffee cake and Everett once more lackadaisically aligning Chief Henderson's tomes on the workings of the judicial system, Sergeant Putnam sat at his desk and tried to imagine what, in this situation, Len would do, knowing that Len wouldn't just sit and ponder implications and probabilities. No, he'd slap on his cap, pop up to Orianna's Colonial palace, deliver an avuncular address pointing out the folly of her avowed course of action, and, with duty and conscience satisfied, let the matter take its course.

Somehow, Sergeant Putnam could not picture himself in an avuncular role. While no date of birth had crept into Orianna's press releases, it was accepted fact among Hampfordites that she had already passed the age of forty, whereas Sergeant Putnam was still two years short of this milestone. In fact, in Orianna's presence he reverted to adolescence. Her extravagant taste, her constant dramatizing, were repugnant to his New England sensibilities, yet his reaction to these traits struck him as gauche. What he found particularly unsettling was her air of quiet amusement. What the hell was amusing? His bulk? His big feet? His earnest freckled face? Oh shit, he said to himself as he got up and reached for his cap. If I were suave, I wouldn't be in Hampford.

He left Everett on duty with the usual admonitions to look alive, keep his greasy fingers off the logbook, and Twinkie crumbs off the counter, and backed the cruiser out of its parking slot. A cold drizzle floated lightly earthward, casting an oily sheen on the macadam and pearling with silver tears the Garden Club's redwood planter, which bore a symmetrical display of somewhat battered, but gallant, orange Kaufmania tulips.

Swinging north on Main Street, he passed the common on his right and the firehouse, the Olde Chestnut Gift Shoppe, and Sonia's Bakery on his left, the latter loyally patronized by Hampford's men in blue. Chief Henderson in particular had a predilection for Sonia's lardy concoctions, which probably accounted for ninety percent of his dyspepsia.

Orianna had purchased the Bertram house on Chapel Road, the last of the Bertrams having had the bad luck to break his hip in a fall at the age of a hundred and two. The house had been on the market for over a year by the time Orianna came along, searching for rural gentility, mainly because it needed extensive renovations, old Rufus having possessed neither the strength nor the funds to do more than shove pans under the leaks. Orianna had fallen in love with the mellow, friendly aspect of the dwelling, with its spreading ash and oaks, and had then proceeded with great energy to impose her will upon it and change its face completely. Even the ash was sacrificed when she discovered that every breath of wind sprinkled leaves and twigs across the surface of the pool. Eventually, she had straightened and stiffened and squared the old place until it looked like any reproduction Colonial she could have had for half the cost. Sergeant Putnam regretted the loss of charm but was well aware his was a minority opinion. In fact, most of Hampford's citizens shared Orianna's enthusiasm for "fixing up," and were openly envious of the kidney-shaped pool and the terrace backed with sliding glass doors and the rock garden delivered and installed in the space of an afternoon.

Sergeant Putnam turned into the weed-free gravel driveway and sighed at the sight of emerald lawns and sculpted shrubs. How could he avoid comparing, to his dissatisfaction, the gleaming sward in front of him with his own scuffed turf, which was alternately employed as soccer and football field, or Orianna's fatly budded azaleas with his own lean specimens bearing carelessly abandoned bicycles in their burdened branches?

Ruefully surveying the fruits of affluence, he parked in front of a garage the size of a cottage and advanced toward the back of the house. Now, however, an impressive sun porch was superimposed between himself and the main structure, and while he hesitated, wondering not only where to gain entrance but whether mid-morning was, after all, the right time to call on authors, Orianna appeared on the other side of the glass and beckoned him somewhat imperiously toward an end panel, where he discovered a brass knob.

"I thought you were the man with my car," she said, giving the impression that had she known otherwise she would have bolted the door.

The porch, with its meticulous coordination of wicker, cushions, rugs, and drapes, resembled a department store showroom. Sergeant Putnam looked in vain for some small token of Orianna's individuality, but even the plants seemed mass-produced.

"I'd like to talk to you, if I may."

"We can sit here," Orianna replied, none too graciously. The plushly carpeted sanctum beyond the porch was obviously off limits to his grass-spattered shoes, but the sun room was comfortably warm, despite the grayness of the day. He sat down gingerly on a flat blue-cushioned white wicker armchair, conscious of the mud on his cuffs, and Orianna sat on the sofa opposite, tucking her legs beneath her like a young girl, which she was not.

She was wearing a pink jogging suit and matching pink sneakers, which Sergeant Putnam, who shared the town's lack of sophistication in such matters, thought rather frivolous garb in which to pursue what he regarded as a somewhat ascetic profession. But then, he reflected, writing was not like "regular" work. Silver bells dangled from her earlobes beneath a cap of sleek black hair. Her face, carefully animated, impressed him with its gaity and youthfulness—a perception belied only when Orianna, alone, let the ensemble sag and, taking a good hard look at herself in the mirror, saw the little lines fanning out from the corners of her eyes and the discontented set of her mouth. Although her bright persona had not for one instant cracked in public, she had experienced, in the last few months, moments verging on panic, as it became apparent that desire alone was not going to produce another book. The heady spate of interviews and talk shows was a thing of the past; bookstore appearances had dwindled to nothing. Except for sporadic invitations to speak at women's clubs and libraries in towns that grew more and more obscure, Orianna had found herself unemployed. Obviously the time had come to sit down and turn out another success. Quite confidently, she retired to her little writing room, where, after several abortive starts, she was forced to consider the awful possibility of creative impotence.

The invitation from the tricentennial committee had come as a godsend, not only enabling her in good conscience to set aside her feeble attempts, but renewing her sense of self-importance, which had so savagely begun to erode. Thus, the amount of opposition encountered at the meeting had been extremely hurtful. Interpreted by her already fragile ego as a personal attack, the evening's criticism had banished any doubts she had harbored—or thought she had harbored— about utilizing material that just might possess enough inherent drama to surmount her own limitations.

Her obvious animosity toward him strengthened Sergeant Putnam's resolve. After all, for all she knew, he might have come collecting for the Police Relief Association. Her hostile reaction confirmed the verdict of guilty as charged in his own mind, and he plunged right in.

"Oh, for God's sake," interrupted Orianna wearily. "Are you going to start on that, too? Scott went nag, nag, nag all the way home."

"Shouldn't that tell you something? You've upset everyone in town who's gotten wind of your intentions."

"In other words, the entire population," Orianna said with a laugh. "I've never heard so much fuss about so little. I do not intend to write an exposé of life in Hampford. Who the hell would read it? I merely said that I might make use of certain events that took place trillions of years ago, names, dates, and locations to be thoroughly camouflaged. What in the name of God is so disturbing about that?"

"It may seem like a trillion years ago to you," Sergeant Putnam explained patiently, "but in a small town, where not much happens, what *does* happen tends to linger from generation to generation. There's no way you could mask the facts effectively. Even if the truth went no farther than this community, it would cause a lot of distress, and realistically, it *would* go farther. Could you resist dropping sly hints, for instance, in one of those talk-show interviews you do, to the effect that your novel was not entirely fiction? Wouldn't that make it more interesting? Sell more books? Bring outsiders snuffling around here, to ferret out the facts? You bet it would. You can also be sure that they'd patronize our tragedies and turn our foibles into amusing yokel anecdotes. We don't need that."

There. The back of his neck was wet. Was he sweating from his own eloquence or the heat of the room? He was aware of Orianna's perfume, which was overpowering and certainly smelled like no common flower of nature.

Studying him in a most disagreeable fashion, she asked coldly, "Is that an ultimatum?"

"Let's call it a friendly word of advice. It's your decision, of course, but if you persist with your present plans, you may find yourself looking for another residence."

"I'd like to see anyone try to run me out."

"Nobody's going to run you out, Mrs. Soule, but the atmosphere could become somewhat unpleasant—surely you can understand that."

"You *are* threatening me," Orianna snapped back, eyes narrowed.

Dammit, he'd done just what he hoped he wouldn't do, he'd made her mad. "I'm thinking of your welfare."

"The hell you are. You're thinking of your own skin, just like everyone else. If you have to placate the fossils of this town, that's your concern, not mine. I got my material from the public library, from sources available to anyone. To tell me I can't use what I've found is outright intimidation, and I will not be bullied."

So now she was a goddamn martyr, thought Sergeant Putnam gloomily. He'd clearly lost whatever chance he might have had to change her mind, if indeed there had ever been a chance. Well, she could stew in her own bile, he concluded peevishly, rising to his feet. He'd delivered the message.

She was smiling at him, now that he was leaving. "What's the matter with that Indian, anyway?" she asked sweetly, mockery in her eyes.

"There's nothing the matter with Merlin."

"You don't find him feverishly aggressive? Goodness, he gave me the shivers."

"Oh, stop it," Sergeant Putnam said irritably, and he

clumped across the gravelled driveway with her laughter at his back.

As his cruiser disappeared around the curve to the road, the amusement faded from Orianna's face and she stared unseeing over her lush rain-spangled acres of lawn. What a nerve he had, tramping into her house in his ugly, muddy shoes to deliver his crude admonition. He *deserved* to be dismissed as comic relief. And yet he had unexpectedly and effectively demeaned her by accentuating her peripheral position in the town's social structure.

The "old" families of Hampford had never extended to Orianna an invitation of any kind, although their members were invariably cordial in casual meetings. The hallowed New England cognomen of Soule they had quickly and with horror ascertained to be pseudonymous, chosen entirely for its euphoniousness, Orianna's maiden name, Mary Agnes Papp, being no more suitable to a book jacket than her married title of Maggie Krumbaecker. Consequently, Orianna had of necessity been drawn into a social circle made up exclusively of new arrivals like herself, and however much they might sneer at those within the magic circle—who appeared, in the main, dowdy, or wacky, or both—any exclusion carries some sting; Orianna was not immune. In fact, had she possessed a little more self-knowledge, she might have realized that her insistence on exploiting Hampford's history was not entirely motivated by professional considerations but also to some degree by the opportunity to strike back at its high and mighty, whose smugness she found absurd. To encounter such hubris in a little town in the middle of nowhere was, to her mind, both surprising and ridiculous.

The truth was, Orianna missed the city. In her headlong rush from Graham's betrayal, she had turned her back on their shared environment as well, having no desire to encounter her ex-husband arm-in-arm with stupid, domesticated Linda in the very spots he and she had once frequented. (It should be noted here that not *one* of Orianna's old friends had a good word to say about Linda; all were *entirely* sympathetic toward Orianna.) And of course Orianna had subsequently proved herself superior to fat Linda, in all respects, with her house and her book and her newly acquired reputation. True, Linda had Graham, but a somewhat seedy Graham, a relaxed and lazy and careless Graham whom Orianna hardly recognized from the descriptions obligingly furnished by their friends. Sunk to *her* level, no doubt, he was hardly something she'd want back, even if he'd wished to come.

Still, the fact remained that, despite their loyalty to Orianna, her old circle now encompassed both Graham *and* Linda, who had slipped in simply through proximity and the passage of time, while Orianna found herself the outcast. It was a strange term to apply to the acknowledged leader of Hampford's jet set, those young professionals from Apple Valley and Spruce Ridge who regarded themselves as the town's trendsetters and zealously sought invitations to Orianna's lively pool parties and terrace gatherings, but the truth was, they were avant-garde only west of Worcester and beginning to bore Orianna very much. The house, now finished, seemed rather flat after the excitement of perfecting it, and she had not dreamed that winters in the country could be so bloody quiet. Furthermore, with her self-esteem rebuilt, she was beginning to feel attractive and desirable and in need of greener pastures once again.

In her present financial state, however, a move was out of the question. All her capital was tied up in her property and would never be entirely recouped, since people with that kind of money, she now realized, did not buy real estate in Hampford. Besides, she didn't really want to lose the house, preferring to maintain it as a symbol of her achievement, while spending the drearier months in a cozy Boston apartment. The proceeds from another best-seller, wisely invested, could very well make possible such a best-of-both-worlds situation, and that best-seller was lying dormant in the notes on her desk. Good God, who in her right mind would throw away such an opportunity? Certainly not Maggie Papp Krumbaecker.

CHAPTER 4

VESTA BOWER WAS FRYING a panful of liver and bacon for her brothers' supper. No quick mixes or frozen dinners defiled the shopping carts of the house-wives of Vesta's generation, who had learned their cooking from scratch, a principle that in Vesta's case was regrettable, since Vesta boiled her vegetables to a mush and fried meat until it curled. Her kitchen was filled with a perpetual greasy blue haze. In fifty years of culinary practice, she had not deviated one iota from her original bungled approach. Quality had never been an issue. Quantity and punctuality were the standards she had learned at her mother's elbow, and Vesta could say truthfully and pridefully that she had never once kept her brothers waiting for their awful meals.

Brother Harley was the wage earner. Every week-day morning at eight-fifteen Harley left the house for his position as a clerk at the county courthouse in Mount Pleasant, where he single-handedly kept the wheels of justice turning. In the eyes of his siblings, Harley belonged on the bench. Vesta ironed his shirts and pressed his suits, dusted their late mother's knick-knacks, and kept the house in which they had been born and raised scrupulously vacuumed and mercilessly polished.

While Harley went off with his brown-bag lunch, Albert cut the grass and hoed the garden, replaced rotting clapboards, and looked after the hens. At one time, many years before, Albert, too, had held a job, but that left the grass uncut. Harley's salary proved sufficient to sustain them all as long they practiced economy—any other way of life being, in any case, unthinkable. The house, preserved in the Bower family through five generations, had taken on the aspect of a shrine, and the siblings' greatest anxiety was its disposition after their lifetimes. Only Margaret, of the four of them, had married and gone away, and she was dead now thirty-six years, drowned on her wedding trip, as though in retribution for her audacity. Ma and Pa had grown old, were cared for, and passed on. The Bowers found themselves middle-aged, settled, locked into their respective roles. The town, as well, tended to regard the Bowers as a unit.

It was also inclined to label them elderly, which was not, in fact, the case, although all three had turned gray prematurely. Harley, the eldest, was a mere sixty-four, a year away yet from retirement, and the most worldly of the trio, having served with the Seabees in the

28

Second World War. Vesta was a year younger, and Albert, the baby, was only fifty-eight and bore such an ingenuous expression that he appeared as ageless as a wood gnome. He and Vesta took after their mother and the rest of the Spragues, being short and wiry, with pale startled-looking blue eyes and frizzy little halos of gray fluff. Harley, on the other hand, was a true Bower, tall and lean, with deep eye sockets, small, sharp eyes, and a beaky nose.

Arriving home at precisely five o'clock, Harley would drive his car directly into the shelter of the barn, a typically cautious Bower practice, and there the vehicle would remain until the following morning, unless it happened to be a Wednesday, which was Harley's night for prayer meeting. He had some six years previously, to the great unvoiced distress of his siblings, inexplicably left the Congregational Church to join a group called the Tabernacle of the New Jerusalem. Since he did not discuss his apostasy, his motivation remained unclear. He stood aloof from the abandon of his fellow worshippers; his ecstasy level was right down at the bottom of the scale. Yet even as a mere onlooker, he appeared to derive a degree of fulfillment from the proceedings that had escaped him in the austere setting of the Congregationalists.

On this evening, as he did every evening, he entered the house through the kitchen door, nodded to his sister, and went upstairs to change his clothes. They were not a family for small talk. In the large front bedroom that had been his mother and father's for the fifty-three years of their married life, he hung up his blue suit, put his white shirt in the hamper, and after pulling on an old pair of slacks, a frayed dress shirt, and a cardigan patched with leather at the elbows, he descended to the kitchen.

Albert had finished feeding the hens and was waiting expectantly in his place with shiny face and dampened hair. Like actors in a long-running play, the Bowers moved from spot to spot and task to task with perfect timing. The brothers sat, Vesta placed their plates before them, filled her own, took her seat, and removed her linen napkin from the pewter kitty with the basket that had been hers since childhood. Harley had inherited Pa's hollowed ring of hickory and Albert had a china dog with a bow tie. They bowed their gray heads as Harley asked the blessing. Vesta was relieved every evening to hear the same simple words that their father had mumbled over *his* pot roast and fried scrod, living, as she did, in fearful expectation of the evening when Harley would throw up his arms and recite some New Jerusalem gibberish. But Harley had so far contained himself, if indeed that was his impulse.

He ate slowly and thoughtfully, with an amazing amount of appreciation for his dry slab of liver with its garnish of undercooked bacon and limp fried onions, this gastronomic delight accompanied by cooling boiled carrots and gummy egg noodles. Albert consumed his portion a little more hurriedly, his hunger honed by his outdoor tasks, and Vesta took her nourishment piecemeal, bobbing up from time to time to refill the bread dish or fetch Harley a glass of water or press upon Albert another spoonful of carrots.

"I heard something today." Harley announced at last, and let their expectation mount while he cleaned his plate with half a slice of bread. Vesta put down her fork and devoted her entire attention to her brother. There had been a gravity to his tone that seemed to portend a pronouncement of some importance.

"Walter McPhee came into court," Harley told them, "on that business between Cleon Wimble and himself about their property line, and of course Judge Sawyer was an hour late."

Harley did not approve of Judge Sawyer, whom he considered frivolous. His loyalty, and therefore the loyalty of his siblings, went to old Judge Fogg, who did not allow himself to fall behind schedule, even if it meant chopping off a case half-heard.

"So naturally Walter sat and talked with me. It's a good thing I can work while I listen."

Secretly, of course, he reveled in these interruptions, just as he reveled in the necessity of enlightening his fellow townsmen who wandered bewildered into the courthouse and turned to him as the one who knew the ropes. Vesta and Albert shared his sense of importance vicariously. Goodness knows what would happen to American justice without Harley in charge. Neighbors might lose themselves forever in the cold marble halls of the Third District Court, Judge Fogg search in vain for his briefings, Judge Sawyer fall hopelessly and irrevocably out of touch.

"The pageant committee met last night, as you know," Harley continued.

Of course they knew. They were right on top of the anniversary happenings. Harley was a member of the steering committee, Albert in charge of the Poultry Breeder's float, and Vesta was working on the tricentennial quilt that was to be raffled off at the pancake breakfast.

"It seems there was a bit of a ruckus over Mrs.

Soule's script, which, you may remember, is just what I predicted. I believe I said asking an outsider to write about us is asking for trouble."

"Yes, that's what you said," Vesta agreed.

"It seems she lost her temper," Harley informed them gravely. "She told Scott Coffin, who drove her home, that she had done a lot of research for that script and had accumulated a lot of facts about the history of this town and might very well disguise those facts as fiction and publish them in a book. But, of course," he added bleakly, seeing Vesta's face go quite gray, "no disguise would be adequate."

"After all these years," Vesta said quaveringly.

"The bitch," said Albert.

"No, Albert, you mustn't," Vesta said, distress obvious.

"But she is, Vesta. She's a bitch."

"Albert, please."

"We must not allow ourselves to panic," Harley said heavily. "Her project may never get beyond the stage of talk. Still, we must keep our ears open and stay abreast of the situation and pray that her intentions die a natural death."

"Yes, it may be a false alarm," Vesta concurred.

But all three Bowers were thoroughly shaken and sat lost in thought for some minutes before Vesta rose to clear away the dinner plates and bring on the blackened gingerbread.

CHAPTER 5

GILBERT COFFIN, WITH THE help of his son Scott, was building a brick barbeque pit in his backyard at the edge of the flagstone terrace that he had laid two years before. So few had there been of either dry or warm weekend days, that the structure was still more vision than fact. But on this Sunday afternoon the sun was shining intermittently at last, drawing out of the warming earth a strong odor of fresh wet soil. Coarse new grass sparkled brightly in the lawn, and along the side of the garage King Alfred daffodils stood in rows like good soldiers, nodding their yellow heads.

Scott and his father wore lumber jackets, work

gloves, and heavy boots, having changed after church and dinner. Scott had never challenged his parents' way of life, accepting it as right and decent. He was just a little too wholesome to seem quite real. An Eagle Scout at sixteen, a modest athletic hero at his high school and a model student, but not *too* intelligent, not brilliant or creative or unconventional or any of those distressing things, he had maintained his admirable normality through Amherst and, with a smugness that was forgiveable because it was entirely sincere, had decided to dedicate his life to molding young minds. With master's degree in hand, he applied for an opening at his alma mater, Valley Regional, where he had now spent five, on the whole successful, years, teaching Modern World and American histories and coaching both football and hockey.

His father, who busily applied *his* energies to the manufacture and marketing of Berkshire Potato Chips, thought Scott had the stuff for medical school and was distressed to see him enter what he regarded as a second-rate profession. But, in common with most parents, he came in time not only to accept the accomplished act, but to find certain consequences of his son's decision gratifying. He liked the fact that Scott still lived at home and shared many of his own interests. Who among his contemporaries could boast of such a companionable relationship? And despite the fact that Valley Regional's athletic teams rarely surpassed the rather mediocre standards of the school as a whole, Gil was a loyal rooter at all of Scott's games.

Scott's adolescence had thus, in a sense, been prolonged, and since he had lived an all-American, clean-cut adolescence, the situation was acceptable not only to Gilbert Coffin, but to the whole family as well. Scott respected his mom, fetched lap robes for Grandma, and tossed a football with Terry, his retarded brother. Two sisters had left home with some alacrity at eighteen, one for college and one for Barbizon, but they showed up on holidays and always seemed happy to see everyone, for a short time, at least. Both lived in Boston. Tracy, the aspiring model, taught aerobics in a health club, and Lisa, who had gone to Simmons, worked as a buyer for T.J. Maxx. She did not take seriously her mother's suggestion that she move back home and apply for a job at J.C. Penney in the Mount Pleasant Mall.

On this typical Sunday, Scott and Terry had accompanied their parents and grandmother to their customary pew in the Congregational Church, where Terry had held the hymnal upside down and Grandma repeatedly dropped her gloves. Then home they'd driven, appetites ready, to a meal of roast chicken and apple pie. Now, Mom was washing the dishes, Grandma was napping, Terry was watching TV wrestling, and Dad and Scott were making a neat job of the barbecue pit while picturing the happy occasions this new addition would provide.

On the surface, a day like so many other days, but underneath the surface strange currents flowed. The first hint of aberrancy had appeared Thursday night. Scott had come home with news of Orianna's intentions and his dad had gone out and gotten sloshed. Not that the Coffins so labeled his condition, but lack of formal recognition did not alter the facts: for the first time in his life, Scott saw his father drunk. Mrs. Coffin was not able to shield her boy, for Gilbert tangled himself in his trousers while attempting to undress and fell heavily to the bedroom floor, a position from which his wife was unable to raise him unaided. Naturally no one alluded to the incident the following morning, for it was not the Coffins' practice to dwell on unpleasantries, but even a gallant application of will could not deny Gilbert's preoccupation with his own heavy thoughts.

Now he said casually, busily applying mortar to a row of bricks, "Heard any more about this Orianna Soule business?"

"I heard that Dave Putnam went up to talk to her, but she was not very receptive. She doesn't feel she owes us anything."

"She ought to be horsewhipped."

"Jeez, Dad," Scott said with a laugh, a little unsettled by the intensity of his father's feelings. "Let her write what she wants. We've got nothing to hide."

"Scott, I've got to talk to you, man-to-man," his father said solemnly, laying down his trowel. "I've got to talk to someone and I think you're the right one."

"Sure, Dad. Fire away."

"It's about this plan of Mrs. Soule's to make public what she's uncovered. The question is, of course, just what *has* she uncovered? Maybe it's nothing that need concern us, but on the other hand, there is the chance that it could concern us very deeply. I'm going to tell you something that I've never told another soul, not even your mother. But you're the one who will carry on the Coffin name, and I would rather you hear this from me than read about it in some piece of sensational junk."

Scott attended to this preamble with no more than mild curiosity. He had no idea what his father was

36

referring to, but in view of the old man's grave tone and in keeping with his own role as confidant, he did his best to look both sympathetic and intelligent.

"I don't know if you've ever wondered how poor Terry got that way," his father went on.

Scott shrugged. "An accident of conception. A few mixed-up genes."

"I had a brother like Terry," his father continued, disregarding Scott's surmise. "He died young. I had an aunt who was hidden away all her life. I remember going to see her in an attic room. My father told me then that in *his* father's generation there were three of them, Scott. I never told your mother. I was afraid she wouldn't marry me. God, how I prayed before you were born. You were like a miracle, and then Lisa came and she was fine and Tracy just as healthy and normal. I stopped worrying. I laughed at my fears. And then we had Terry."

"It can happen to anyone, Dad. It's all statistics, one out of so many births."

"That's just it, son. Statistically, we're way above average. I've never understood it. A law-abiding, God-fearing, patriotic family. What did we do wrong?"

"You didn't *do* anything, Dad. That kind of thinking is dangerous. You'll be telling me next that we're under some kind of curse."

"It's crossed my mind."

"Hey, come off it. I mean, we all love Terry. It's not the worst thing that can happen. So, okay, in the old days it was shameful—like hiding your aunt away, that's medieval, for God's sake. But Terry lives a full life. He goes to public school, he's accepted in the neighborhood."

"Oh, we've managed and Terry's managed. But think what our life would be like if we didn't have him, or if he were normal. It's been an awful strain on your mother; it still is. And he'll be your responsibility when we're gone. What I'm saying, Scott, is sure, a family can have a retarded kid and still have a pretty good life, but no one would *choose* it. Why do you think I didn't tell your mother about my aunt or my great-aunts or my great-great-uncle? I was afraid, that's why, and now I'm afraid for you. You've been going with Robyn Wright for three years. She's a nice girl, from a good family. We'd be very happy, your mother and I, to see you marry Robyn. But she's not at ease with Terry. You know that as well as I do. What do you think she'd say if she knew there was a good chance she'd have a Terry of her own? Do you think she'd marry you? Do you think anyone would? I can't tell you how important it is to me to see another generation of Coffins, and it's up to you to produce them, Scott."

The two men were standing face-to-face across the forgotten barbecue pit, Gilbert still holding a brick. Scott, for all his glib rebuttals of his father's suppositions, was more shaken than he cared to admit. Gil's introduction of Robyn had transformed the issue from theoretical to personal. Robyn was not *uneasy* with Terry, as his father had diplomatically put it, she was downright repulsed. It made her miserable that she felt that way, but she couldn't help herself. Like some people, she explained to Scott, had an unreasoning horror of spiders or snakes or rats. Of course, nowadays you didn't just have to take what you got. They had some kind of test, didn't they, that could tell a woman if she was carrying a defective child? But what then? He and Robyn had been raised to sanctify the product of conception as God's handiwork.

Damn, thought Scott. Children were an integral part of Robyn's concept of marriage. Forced to choose between himself and a family, he was not at all certain what her choice would be. Besides, he didn't want a Terry any more than Robyn did. He already had a Terry, a Terry who was going to be his for life somewhere down the road.

"I'm sorry, son," his father said sadly, as though following Scott's train of thought.

"That's okay, Dad. You had to tell me sooner or later," Scott answered bravely. But he wondered if he hadn't perhaps gotten the worst of it. His father, living in dread of exposure, was seeking to protect both the past and the present. Whether Orianna wrote her book or not, Scott bore the burden of the future.

CHAPTER 6

SERGEANT PUTNAM APPROACHED THE following Thursday's meeting of the pageant committee with a mixture of complacency and trepidation. His cheerfulness sprang from the knowledge that Chief Henderson would occupy his usual seat at the next encounter; his uneasiness was the consequence of his experiences during and after the last meeting. Myron, appearing to share his sense of foreboding, had thrown open the windows, as if to cool down any impending altercations. The weather, in that month of extremes, had turned warm overnight, and the breeze wafting through the room carried intoxicating odors of moist earth and cold rushing water. Laurel and Scott were chatting pleas-

41

antly, and Bea welcomed Sergeant Putnam with a wave and a smile. She looked very frail, seated between Myron and Scott. Bea would never admit to weakness, having been raised in an era when Spartan attitudes were strongly encouraged, but her willingness to serve her town in any capacity, however humble, had long been exploited.

Merlin arrived with a large manila envelope and a belligerent expression, and they all sat and waited for Orianna. The group's natural impulse was, of course, to dive right into a lively discussion of her conduct, but, fearing her imminent arrival, they felt unnaturally constrained. Thus, the forbidden topic was determinedly circumvented, and the resultant tension had built to an uncomfortable level by the time Orianna materialized, fifteen minutes late, in a bright-red jersey dress and eye shadow so heavy she seemed to be peering out of two purple plums.

"Well, here we are again," she said brightly, encompassing the gathering with a warm smile.

Was this the fearful specter who had haunted their week? Was it possible that this sunny soul had threatened them? Or had they mistaken ignorance for malignancy? Into the somewhat uneasy silence, Myron proposed that they get down to business.

"Have you come up with a few suggestions, Merlin?"

Merlin squared a pile of papers on the tabletop in front of him. At the sight of these "few" suggestions, glazed expressions spread over the faces of the committee members, with the exception of Orianna, who was all hovering interest. She was *agog*, she assured Merlin encouragingly, to hear what he had to say. In the face of such determined sweetness, Merlin found it impossible to maintain his animosity. He apologized gruffly for losing his temper; Orianna apologized for losing hers. Myron exercised his executive expertise and brought Merlin back to the business at hand.

Merlin, it transpired, had not only rewritten the scene on the common, he had rewritten history. The settlers in his script were a sorry lot, sneaky, dishonest, hirsute little creatures as dark and mean as their wretched cabins. Displaying an abysmal ignorance of forest lore, they were rescued from certain starvation by the magnanimity of the Wompanakis, who were, to a man, six feet tall, gracious, brave, handsome, and pure. Joseph Handy had been demoted out of sight and the lead role awarded to Running Bird, a noble chief of the tribe. Nor was there any mention of a roasted ox. In Merlin's account, the Englishmen were gnawing acorns when Running Bird and his villagers arrived bearing a five-course meal.

"CHIEF RUNNING BIRD: (*Speaking decent colloquial English.*) Hello there, people, we've brought a few little items that we'll never eat up—bear and deer, rabbits, turkeys, grouse, ducks and pheasants, all manner of excellent fruit, tasty berries, corn, pumpkins, beans, and many other gifts of nature's bounty. Take what you can use.

"PELETIAH BIRDLIME: How can we ever thank you enough, Chief Running Bird? Truly, it is due to the generosity of the Wompanakis that we have survived. We will repay your kindness with treachery and deceit, but that comes later. Today let's have a decent meal, our first in weeks."

Myron coughed. It wasn't necessary for Orianna to say a word. Instead, she simply looked down at her lap and smiled ever so slightly when Myron suggested that Merlin's version, while very interesting, might be just a little subjective, as partisan perhaps in its point of view as was Orianna's at the other end of the spectrum. Couldn't they just get something in the *middle*?

It did not, alas, seem possible. As the discussion dragged on, Myron began to see the whole pageant disappearing down the road—and his reputation with it. He lost his patience and banged his fist on the table.

"Now listen here," he shouted, "if you don't come to some kind of agreement in the next five minutes, I'll write the damn thing myself."

"Oh, fine," said Orianna. "A pig's-eye view of the Civil War."

With that, all hope of settlement flew out the window. Myron, as a business executive and chairman of the board of selectmen, was accustomed to fairly deferential treatment. He had, in fact, reached the point some time ago of assuming as a personal tribute, the respect accorded his positions, a misconception his wife Doris unwittingly reinforced by referring to him both privately and publicly as "Boss Man." In other words, a great many years had passed since Myron had been the recipient of a deliberate insult, and now Myron was purple. Scott, attempting to lighten the atmosphere with a bright remark, was told quite rudely to shut up.

"If a certain person remains on this committee," Myron continuted through clenched teeth, "this committee will lose its chairman."

There was no need for heroics, Orianna assured him lightly, gathering up her script. She had wasted all the time she could afford to waste. If and when they decided to take her seriously, she would consider returning. In the meantime, she had other, more important things to do.

And with that, she vanished through the doorway, leaving her fellow committee persons looking slightly stunned—all, that is, except Merlin, who seemed to be waging some sort of inner struggle. Suddenly, he shuffled his papers together and jumped to his feet.

"On behalf of the Wompanaki people, I say your approach is full of crap. You decide to tell the truth and I'll be back. Otherwise, forget it."

And then he, too, was out the door.

"Well, at least we know where we stand," said Myron, who had calmed down. "Anyone else want to leave? I guess we're going to have to come up with something ourselves."

"I don't think that's impossible," said Bea stoutly, and indeed, with the two principal antagonists out of the way, some kind of resolution seemed, for the first time, a real possibility.

The surface affability, however, only thinly disguised the haunting disquiet that had settled in the room. Orianna's insult had casually, familiarly, made use of knowledge held inviolable by common consent. She had broken an unspoken law of small-town life and done it, apparently, without a moment's compunction. What manner of impudence might she undertake for her own benefit if she understood and cared so little about the proprieties of her environment? Alas, no doubt remained in anyone's mind that she was fully capable of unmercifully revealing their every wart.

CHAPTER 7

FRIDAY STARTED BADLY AND soon got worse. Sergeant Putnam awoke to find Barbara sitting at his elbow, commiserating into a bedside telephone.

"You tell him not to worry, Catherine. Everything's fine here. Dave will be waiting to hear from you. I hope it's good news. . . . I said, I hope it's good news."

"Oh, God," groaned Sergeant Putnam, as his wife replaced the receiver, "is that what I think it is?"

"Len had one of his attacks last night, a really bad one. They had to rush him to the hospital in New Haven. They're going to run some tests today. His little ménage is all aflutter."

"Dammit," the sergeant said, "a few more hours and he would have got home."

"How inconsiderate of him."

"Thoughtless," her husband agreed, "considering he's now stuck in a decent hospital instead of muddled old Mount Pleasant. He'll be lucky to get home for the Tricentennial."

"You are a Gloomy Gus this morning. Was I wrong to tell Catherine that everything's fine?"

"It's fine enough," Sergeant Putnam said, without much conviction.

Nature, as though to mock his misfortune, had produced a shining morning. He crossed the common against a gentle breeze, beneath the softened outlines of the maples. On the dew-wet grass a robin danced, engaged in a tug-of-war with a recalcitrant worm. So what if Len wasn't back today, he asked himself. Was the world going to stop? Nothing had happened beyond the exchange of a few harsh words and that was hardly a novelty. Why, there were feuds in town that had simmered for decades. Still, he couldn't rid himself of the prickly premonition that his feet were planted on sliding sand.

Ted was hanging up the phone when Sergeant Putnam walked into the station, a station as shiny as the day. The town map that had been curling at the edges was firmly reattached to the back wall, the ashtrays washed, the chairs aligned.

"Whew," said Ted, with something close to admiration, "that Mrs. Soule is one angry lady."

"Who did you say?"

"Mrs. Orianna Soule. Somebody threw a rock through her window last night."

48

No surprise attended this revelation, but Sergeant Putnam was dismayed that his presentiment had so quickly proven valid.

"Anyone hurt?"

"Not a person, Dave, but nevertheless a living thing. The rock was thrown through a window of her glass porch and knocked a potted sansevieria off a table. Broke the window and the pot."

"I'll run right over."

"Gee, I'd like to see her big house," Ted said wistfully.

"You know I'd take you in a minute, Ted, if we weren't so shorthanded. Everything else under control?"

"Affirmative."

Sergeant Putnam paused with his hand on the doorknob to relay the news of Chief Henderson's hospitalization, and Ted made all the appropriate responses, including sympathetic tongue clucking and several shakes of his gray head.

"You can't say I didn't warn him."

You certainly could not. Ted was a vocal proselytizer of his own healthful life-style. He pursued a regimen of simple exercises, tasty balanced meals, and restful slumber, as well as the diligent avoidance of any hint of responsibility and its accompanying stress.

Orianna's ornamental Japanese cherry had bloomed in a cascade of pink froth, and a sheet of scillas had spread a cobalt lake at the edge of the woods since Sergeant Putnam's last visit. Reluctantly forsaking the peaceful splendors of the garden, he turned toward the desecrated porch. Wow, he thought, that was no piece of gravel. A hole the size of a Grade-A Florida grapefruit gaped in the panel nearest the driveway, and from it radiated a spidery web of cracks that reached almost to the frame in every direction. A missile launched with fervor, was the sergeant's wry conclusion.

Orianna met him at the door—a tight-lipped Orianna who wordlessly waved her hand at the floor. He crunched through the shards of glass, appraising the damage. A fractured pot lay on the rug with the root ball of a lacerated sansevieria exposed. Beyond an area strewn with glass splinters, the rock had come to rest against the leg of an armchair, a nice chunky piece of granite, plucked, more than likely, off a handy stone wall. Beneath Orianna's sardonic gaze, he slipped the evidence into a plastic bag.

"Have any idea when this happened?"

"No, I don't. My bedroom is at the front of the house."

"Was there a note?"

"On a rock?"

"Wrapped around it."

"I hardly think a note was necessary, do you? The message is clear enough. I'd like to know what you're going to do to keep this kind of thing from happening again."

"I think that's mostly up to you."

"Police protection is not a privilege," Orianna said through clenched teeth, "to be earned with good behavior. It's my right whether you like me or not. I pay taxes in this town and I expect some kind of responsible response to this assault."

Because there was more than a kernel of truth in her censure, it was all the harder to listen to, for above all else, Sergeant Putnam dreaded an accusation of lack of professionalism. His reply, given out of necessity, would only reinforce her conviction that he was making moral—she might even say self-righteous—judgments.

"There's frankly not a lot I can do, Mrs. Soule. We're particularly short-handed right now, with the chief away, but even if he were here, we still wouldn't have the manpower for anything like round-the-clock surveillance. Isn't there someone who could stay with you at night? How about your cleaning woman, Verlyn Taggert?"

"What the hell could Verlyn do that I can't do?"

"Your gardener then."

"I have a landscaping service."

"Friends," he persisted.

"Sorry, Sergeant, I am not going to ask anyone else to do your job. If you can't help me, I'll take care of myself."

"You're doing very well at that, aren't you?" he snapped back, his patience with the whole lamentable business exhausted. He was both angry with the misguided townsman who had performed this act of violence, for he had a policeman's horror of personal vendettas, and impatient with Orianna's stubborn resistance to good advice, his own in particular. At the same time, he could not help but grudgingly admire her courage. Her reaction seemed to be wholly one of annoyance. He would have expected, with her writer's imagination, that she might have pictured some pretty gruesome possible sequels to a thrown rock, but if she had, she wasn't revealing her fear.

"Oh, go along," she said rudely, showing him the door. He might even have picked up the pot if she hadn't been so nasty.

For another five minutes he wandered around behind the house, studying the lawn. Two days of sun had dried the ground and there were no helpful footprints, no discarded cigarette packs, not a match or a button or a toothpick, nothing but green grass and jonquils. The property was unfenced, running into woods along its rear boundary. Evergreen trees and shrubs hid Orianna's neighbors on the left. Of the house on the right, he could make out the corner of a roof, a chimney, and an attic window. In the hope that one of its residents had been peeking from the attic in the dead of night, he went to call. He even tried the house across the street, though he doubted if as much as Orianna's lights showed through the thick hedges of blue spruce that guaranteed her privacy. No one in the neighborhood had noticed or heard a thing, and why should they? The rock thrower had undoubtedly come on foot, slipping through the woods and across the dark lawn, just as any sensible rock thrower would have done.

Sergeant Putnam mulled over possible courses of action while returning to the station and came up with few. He would, as a matter of course, send the rock to the state police lab for fingerprinting, although even a set of the clearest prints would do him no good without a suspect to which to match them. And there was the rub. As far as he knew, half the town was suspect. Why, he had himself witnessed some very angry reactions to Orianna's avowed intentions. Who was to say how many he had not witnessed? His best bet, ignoble as it sounded, was to hope for an informant who, wittingly or otherwise, could provide him with a lead.

Just after noon an urgent call came in for Ted. It seemed the Plummers' pet donkey had escaped from its paddock for the third time in a month and was ambling down Main Street. Ted, who was the local Dr. Doolittle, slapped on his cap and left for the roundup. Donkey cases were invariably time-consuming, and Sergeant Putnam was forced to call in Everett to man the desk when Mrs. Coombs of Liberty Circle reported that a "sinister-looking" man was emerging from her neighbors' house—they were both at work—with a TV set in his arms. Now he was looking right at her windows! Ten minutes later, Sergeant Putnam apologized to a startled son-in-law doing his wife's folks a favor. Mrs. Coombs remained blatantly skeptical. She said she would feel his rapist's eyes on her for a week.

Sergeant Putnam had barely returned to the station and a foil-wrapped packet of baloney sandwiches when Myron Streeter strode in, looking every inch a small-town executive in a discretely patterned gray suit, pale blue shirt, and red tie sprinkled with tiny golf clubs. Everett swallowed two-thirds of a Snickers bar in one gulp and swept a Spiderman comic book off the counter, which alerted Sergeant Putnam to the presence of royalty. He hastened to the front of the room, inviting Myron to take a chair beside the water-marked coffee table. Myron scrutinized the seat before lowering his light gray rump upon it. In one quick perusal, he took in every inch of the room, but Ted, God bless him, had spent the morning dusting and polishing.

"What have you heard from Len? I talked to Catherine yesterday but she was pretty vague."

"They're still testing."

"We know what *that* means," said Myron significantly.

Sergeant Putnam, who didn't, declined to commit

himself to either a smile or a frown and nodded wisely instead.

"Does he know anything about this business with Orianna?"

"I haven't been able to talk to him."

"You're saying he knows nothing about it?"

"I haven't been able to talk to him, Myron."

Myron assumed an expression of infinite sufferance. He knew, of course, about the rock thrown through Orianna's window. The whole of Hampford knew about the rock. There was a general feeling that she had gotten what she deserved, and since this is seldom the case in life, a sense of smug satisfaction at finding a little order in this imperfectly ordered world had descended on the town.

"Have you talked to Orianna?" he asked.

"Of course I've talked to Orianna. I spoke with her this morning and pointed out that we cannot give her permanent police protection."

"Why did you tell her that? What if the Boston papers get hold of this? A well-known author refused protection?"

"Boston papers or not, Myron, there is no way the three of us can be stretched any farther. We've got Beany Bruce doing some night shifts, but even with his help I haven't had a day off since Len left."

"Dave, I realize that, and I appreciate your dedication. The town could not be in safer hands. Believe me, I'm not here to criticize. I'm just wondering out loud, as it were, if there is some way we could make it *look* as though we're protecting her. Frankly, between you, me, and the gatepost, I don't give a tinker's damn what

54

happens to Ms. Orianna Soule. But we've got to give an *appearance* of caring."

"I'll do what I can."

"I'm sure you will."

Myron rose with a smile that never reached his eyes. Everett, who was nobody's fool, rushed to open the door.

"By the way, Dave, any leads on our rock thrower?"

"Not yet," Sergeant Putnam said curtly. "I'll keep you informed."

"That's a good idea, Dave. Len and I have always had excellent communication."

Everett saw Myron out, standing smartly at attention, then gave him the finger behind his back and turned with a wink for Sergeant Putnam.

"What kind of aura does our generalissimo have?" Sergeant Putnam asked grimly, moving back to his desk.

"Solid gold," said Everett, unwrapping another Snickers bar.

The remainder of the afternoon passed serenely on the surface, small problems dealt with efficiently as they arose, but Sergeant Putnam was conscious of a sense of unease. In the absence of any concrete strategy, he found excuses to drive up Chapel Road several times during the course of his shift, which action served no practical purpose whatsoever but comforted him with the illusion that he was keeping an eye on things.

What he needed was Len—Len in his reproduction captain's chair behind his reproduction Colonial desk, covering all available surfaces, vertical or horizontal, with pipe tobacco and cigarette ash while he chewed over the facts and contemplated the options. But Len remained a prisoner of Yale-New Haven Hospital. Catherine called at seven-thirty, just as Sergeant Putnam got home. The test results were inconclusive. Len was going to have to remain another day or two. Meanwhile, the girls would be heading back to Hampford tomorrow to take up their various humble positions, rather a daring move on the girls' part, thought Sergeant Putnam, who could picture them clustered in their motel room in high-necked nightgowns chattering in nervous excitement.

At quarter of ten he was half-heartedly watching a Celtics' game in the living room. Barbara had already gone upstairs, and he was ruminating upon his compulsion to make one last patrol up Chapel Road when he heard the roar of David Junior arriving home in his treasured Mustang. Davey was working afternoons at Seidler's Apothecary and pouring every cent he earned into his first car. As yet, his funds had not extended to a new muffler.

Unlike his brother Tom, who rattled window panes when he shut a door, Davey was so quiet and economical in his movements that Sergeant Putnam looked up to find him already sprawled on the couch.

"Hey, listen, Dad, you can stop worrying about Mrs. Soule. She's all set."

In answer to his father's raised eyebrows, Davey explained.

"Tim Twomey was over to Steve's tonight. He, like, works for her, you know, after school and Saturdays, like he washes the car and cleans the windows. So he's up there this afternoon, he's painting shutters, and she comes out and she says, 'I'd like you to walk Prince.'

And Tim says, 'Prince who?' And then she drags out this humungous Doberman, and that's Prince. So the dog is very well-behaved, like it heels and everything, but when it heels, those big white teeth are right beside Tim's leg, see, and this Prince, he's dancing along and every once in awhile he pulls his lips back, you know, just for the hell of it, and poor old Tim, he almost shit his pants. I know you don't like that expression, but that's how it was."

"A Doberman," Sergeant Putnam mused. "That can be a lot of dog to handle."

"He's trained to attack on command," Davey told him cheerfully.

"For God's sake."

"Anyone comes around that house again, they'll get a legful of teeth."

"Is that what she said?"

"It's what she meant."

"Where the hell did she get this dog?"

"There's plenty of places where you can get them, Dad, trained and everything."

"I suppose there are. And I suppose in her shoes I would have done something too. Maybe we ought to be grateful she bought a dog instead of a gun. Is there any talk at the high school about this book of Mrs. Soule's?"

"Not about her *book*," Davey said, with delicate emphasis on the last word.

"About what then?"

"About who she's making it with."

Sergeant Putnam laughed. "I've heard a few of our elder citizens give voice to the same speculation."

Encouraged by his father's man-to-man acceptance, Davey expanded. "Tim thought she must be needing it pretty bad, so he kind of hinted around a couple of times, but she didn't take him up on it. She must have somebody else."

"She certainly must if she turned down Tim," Sergeant Putnam agreed solemnly.

CHAPTER 8

BY THE FOLLOWING MORNING the "humungous" Doberman had become Hampford's chief topic of conversation. Orianna's action had inspired a certain amount of reluctant admiration in most circles. Spunk in the enemy can also be acknowledged. George Tower, the pharmacist, having owned a series of Dobermans, was cast in the role of oracle, but George proved disappointingly unemotional, asserting that Dobermans were like any other breed: some individual d gs were good, some bad.

Much more satisfactory to the town in its present mood was Emery Gould, Hampford's handyman, who had in the course of his odd-job employment, endured fearsome encounters with dogs of all pedigrees. A Doberman, Emery was now telling his audience, made the hair stand right up on his neck. One time, honest to God, he was trapped in a garden shed for two hours by a slavering fang-toothed fiend so desperate for Emery's flesh that he gnawed at the door boards.

Bea Lambert shook her head. She was one of a small crowd gathered around Emery on the sidewalk outside Seidler's Apothecary on this overcast Saturday morning. Next to Bea stood little Vesta Bower, clutching a sack of cold remedies. Poor Harley had picked up spring congestion.

"The last time I heard that story, Emery Gould," said Bea, "the dog was a German shepherd."

His listeners—Millie Freeman and Analie Stover, Harry Mugford and old Elmer Armstrong, who had paused on his morning constitutional—laughed as much at themselves as at Emery, and the circle broke up as they wandered back to their duties, real or imagined.

Bea fell into step beside Vesta, since they were headed in the same direction. A gusty northeast wind bowed the Sweet Charity daffodils in the window boxes of Jack Dickeman's real estate office, and Vesta clutched a worn black coat around her spare frame. Bea, who was wearing a cardigan, blessed the good sense that had prevented her from a premature removal of her snuggies.

"I'm sorry to hear that Harley is indisposed. Please give him my regards."

To Bea's surprise, Vesta's face flushed and she muttered angrily, "He can't afford to be ill in his position, a position of such responsibility."

"This up-and-down weather being what it is . . . "

60

"It's not the weather," Vesta retorted impatiently. "It's the worrying."

And with that enigmatic statement she hurried down the street, leaving Bea to gaze thoughtfully after her.

Sergeant Putnam was doing some worrying of his own. His gloomy prophecies had proven legitimate, their accuracy confirmed by Catherine in the early morning hours. Len was at this very moment in the process of losing his gall bladder, and Sergeant Putnam was distressed both by his chief's ordeal and by his continued absence. The expectation of time off that had unconsciously buttressed him through the past few days had now receded to some vague future date. Ted was similarly affected and equally depressed, having missed his lodge meeting the previous evening.

"I'll make it up to you later."

"I don't know how you can," Ted said grumpily. "We only have our Polkarama but once a year."

"What the hell is a Polkarama?"

"I wouldn't expect you to know," Ted replied with dignity. "It's good clean fun."

So, Ted was offended and Len was missing and Myron was waiting for him to fall flat on his face and Orianna was challenging the town to come and get her. *Damn!* Cold and raw, the day passed. Ted sulked until he was relieved by Everett, who had a head cold and insisted on wiping his nose on his sleeve.

At four o'clock Sergeant Putnam was called to the scene of a minor auto accident involving two fenders and a lot of shouting. Returning to the station, he pursued a route that was fast becoming an addiction: he swung up Chapel Road. At the top of the hill just before

Orianna's gates, he overtook Tim Twomey in windbreaker and sweatpants trotting beside a prancing Doberman. Sergeant Putnam pulled up next to him and leaned across the front seat to roll down the window. Tim was a handsome, gracefully muscular, cocky kid, with thick black hair and the shadow of a beard, the kind that develops early and not much thereafter. He was cheerfully and totally immersed in himself and not one whit embarrassed by the abysmal ignorance revealed by most of his utterances. He said, "Sit," and the dog sat.

"Seems well behaved," Sergeant Putnam observed.

"Oh, yeah, he's real good."

The dog regarded Sergeant Putnam with opaque ginger-brown eyes. He was a handsome animal, smoothly muscled, his dark coat sleek and rippling.

"How does Mrs. Soule handle him?"

"She don't take no crap. He's like a machine, see. He's not your family pet–type dog, like you don't throw him no sticks and he don't bring no slippers," Tim said, showing a lot of even white teeth in appreciation of his own perception.

Sergeant Putnam went back to the station somewhat reassured. Prince was just a dog, after all, not some kind of monster. Perhaps he was exactly the measure needed to temper the situation. Why wasn't stalemate as legitimate a possibility as escalation? He was further heartened by a message from Catherine. Len had come through surgery very well. He had opened his eyes in the recovery room and whispered faintly, "Tell Dave to get the oil changed in the cruiser." Somehow it was comforting that Len's biggest worry was the state of the cruiser, and Sergeant Putnam went home in a better frame of mind.

Orianna, however, appeared to possess a positive genius for destroying his hard-won moments of peace. Monday morning she did her shopping on Main Street escorted by Prince in a choke collar, and although the dog conducted himself decorously, disdaining, in fact, to take any notice whatsoever of the passersby, Orianna could scarcely have remained oblivious to the current of agitation that followed her progress, a perturbation created in equal measure by Prince as a physical menace and Prince as a symbol of Orianna's defiance. In response to several irate complaints, Sergeant Putnam was forced to walk downtown and confront her, a practice that was becoming repellent, to say the least, since he invariably seemed to come off second-best.

"Sergeant, you are an enigma," Orianna said, smiling up at him with hostile eyes. "First you tell me quite plainly to take care of myself, and now that I've done so, that doesn't suit you either."

"Can you honestly tell me you feel threatened in the middle of Main Street at eleven o'clock on a spring morning?" Sergeant Putnam replied.

"Maybe I'm just parading my insurance," Orianna said coldly, her smile vanishing. "Just so we all know where we stand."

"She's a damn fool," Sergeant Putnam complained later that night to Barbara, "stirring up the pot instead of letting it simmer. Dog or no dog, she's going to get another rock through her window, and I don't know how to stop it."

But Orianna got no more rocks through her windows, for sometime between ten-thirty Monday night and

63

nine o'clock Tuesday morning, Orianna met with a horrible accident, the discovery of which occurred upon Verlyn Taggert's arrival. It was a terrible experience for the poor woman to approach the house, after sloppily parking her rust-spotted Pontiac with its nose in the flowerbed, her mind vaguely concerned with Windex and Noxon, and there to behold, protruding beyond the corner of the porch, a pair of bare feet with coral toenails, and to find, upon further investigation, the rest of Orianna Soule stretched flat on the grass with her mascara smudged and her throat torn out. Verlyn screamed quite involuntarily, and then, averting her eyes from the dreadful wounds, she reached down and gingerly touched one of Orianna's feet, not because she held out any hope of finding Orianna still alive but simply to reassure herself of the reality of the scene. The foot was ice cold and rigid. Verlyn began to shake. Then she turned and stumbled toward her car, shock and nausea supplanted by sheer terror at the realization that the dog was also outside, unless it had opened the door with its clever little paws, an act that did not seem altogether impossible at that point to poor Verlyn. She reached the shelter of the Pontiac, fell into the front seat, fumbled out her key ring, attempted to force the door key into the ignition, sat back and wept. Some two minutes later the Pontiac rolled slowly down the driveway, swung wide at the corner, and crept into the neighboring drive as though the car itself were sick and suffering.

CHAPTER 9

T HE CALL WAS MADE from the Russell house by
Winifred Russell in view of Verlyn's condition, although
Verlyn had recovered enough by that time to appreciate the uniqueness of her position, and with
unconscious anticipation, she readied herself for her
role as premier witness, using Winifred's bathroom
facilities and accepting a cup of well-sweetened coffee.

Sergeant Putnam had awarded to Ted his own
intended free morning as a feeble substitute for the
forfeited Polkarama and was settled for the twelfth
straight day behind his desk when Mrs. Russell's
gruesome tidings poured into his ear. Slamming down
the receiver, he raced after Everett, to whom just

moments earlier he had tossed the cruiser keys along with Chief Henderson's directive concerning the oil, Everett being in the habit of performing the department's routine vehicle maintenance in the backyard of the Hewitt estate, an area plentifully supplied with jacks, greasy mats, and pans of sludge. With Everett positioned behind the wheel, engine running, Sergeant Putnam sprinted back into the station, snatched up the phone, and put through a quick call to Warren Rupert, who was both chief pathologist at the Mount Pleasant Hospital and medical examiner for Wessex County. Then he thundered down the stairs once again, jumped into the front seat next to Everett, and urged him down Main Street toward Chapel Road at a speed that caused old Elmer Armstrong to stop dead in his tracks and lift his cane in a wavering salute.

Everett held off with the observation that the station was unmanned until they were turning onto Orianna's road.

"The hell with the goddamn station," his superior replied grimly, and Everett, whose sentiments often ran along the same lines, experienced a burst of exhilaration that expressed itself in maniacal driving. The cruiser roared up Chapel Road with a squeal of tires and a shower of pebbles. Everett's lips were drawn back in a rictus of pleasure and Sergeant Putnam, who was generally so goddamn *repressive*, never letting him wail the siren or set the old light bar flashing or even *drive*, for godsake, he just sat there and bounced and never said a word.

Everett swung into the Russells' driveway at an angle that seemed destined to deposit the cruiser on top of the Russells' birdbath, but a couple of savage wrenches at the wheel shot them over an azalea and hurtling up the drive with two tires mashing Mr. "Rusty" Russell's neat edging job.

Verlyn had managed to force down a cinnamon roll with her second cup of coffee and was ready to supply Sergeant Putnam with a detailed description of her experiences. She was consequently deeply offended by the sergeant's haste and the brevity of his questions, and only slightly mollified by his instructions that she stay put until his return. If all this enforced hospitality was proving a little wearing to Winnie Russell, she skillfully masked her feelings and joined Verlyn in another cup of coffee. Verlyn had not enjoyed such a leisurely morning in weeks. Mrs. Soule had been fair-minded, she would grant her that, but not *indulgent*.

Everett followed Sergeant Putnam a lot more reluctantly out of the house than he had bounded in. He had a horror of four-legged creatures under the best of circumstances, and Verlyn's description of Mrs. Soule's "tore-out throat" had done little to mitigate his aversion. He proceeded up Orianna's driveway, assiduously studying every prospect except the scene of the tragedy, and ventured a peek at that only when Sergeant Putnam grunted in surprise. The Doberman was crouched over Mrs. Soule's head.

"Jesus, he's eatin' her," Everett screamed.

"Don't be a fool. He's licking her face."

Sergeant Putnam edged himself out of the cruiser and unsnapped his holster. Prince raised his head and whined. As Sergeant Putnam moved forward cautiously, the dog dropped belly to the ground and wiggled backward until his rear end was buried beneath a deutzia gracilis. He rested his head on his paws.

"Whyn't cha plug him right now," Everett begged through the open window of the car. "He's gotta be put down anyways. Next time," he called plaintively, "it might be a little golden-haired child."

Sergeant Putnam appeared unmoved. With his hand still resting on the butt of his revolver, he gazed in solemn reflection at Orianna Soule, or the husk of Orianna Soule, struggling with a vocational proclivity toward the assumption of guilt and the conviction of failure, while experiencing, on a personal level, the shock of a relationship severed with such finality. At the same time, this complex of emotions, however sincere, did not displace his professional curiosity, which, quite without conscious direction, continued to engage part of his mind.

Why had she come outside? Had she heard something? Had Prince heard something? Or was the dog out on his own? He assumed Prince had a bladder like any other dog. Perhaps he hadn't come when she'd called. Perhaps something or someone had distracted him. Orianna had been walking toward the driveway when she was attacked. She was fully dressed, except for her shoes, in jade green velveteen slacks and an off-white cotton sweater. What had she said or done, for godsake, that the dog had interpreted as threatening? Whatever it might have been, the resulting scene was awful to contemplate.

He turned soberly to face the approaching ambulance. Everett, shamed by the arrival of witnesses into abandoning the cruiser, drew near the body at an angle carefully calculated to keep Sergeant Putnam between

68

himself and Prince. The ambulance attendants were no more anxious than Everett to leave their vehicular shelter, but Dr. Rupert, who had followed hard on their heels, shuffled over in his baggy trousers to join the local forces, camera swinging from one hand, medical bag from the other.

"Jesus," he said in shocked summation of the sight before him. "We seem to be getting in the habit of this"—a statement that Sergeant Putnam understood as a reference to violent death in general, rather than to dog attacks in particular. "What are you going to do about *him?*" Dr. Rupert asked, keeping a cautious eye on the shrubbery as he knelt beside the body.

"He'll have to be restrained and examined. Ev, see if the house is open, and if it is, call Beany and tell him to pick up Ted—if Ted's around—and get out here to take the dog. Don't paw through the closets, don't use the bathroom, and stay out of the refrigerator."

"Right, Dave."

The door to the porch swung inward easily under Everett's hand, confirming Sergeant Putnam's surmise that Orianna had spent a casual evening at home. Even had it been her habit to attend social functions barefoot, she wasn't likely to have done so on a chilly spring night.

"Well, what can I say?" Dr. Rupert asked, rising. "He obviously got her right by the throat. She's been dead a good long time. Look at the right arm. See those lacerations down near the wrist? I think she flung that arm up in self-defense. A lot of good it did her, poor thing. And him lying here as cool as a cuke."

"He was licking her face and whining when we arrived."

"No kidding? Dr. Jekyll and Mr. H., eh? I guess I'll

stick to retarded cockers. I suppose you need some shots for the inquest. I'll give you a nice fat set, lots of big glossies. You'll want some good close-ups of the wounds."

Dr. Rupert moved methodically around the body, snapping dispassionately as he went.

"Watch the dog for me, will you? I don't like turning my back to him. You on your own this week?" he asked, with a glance toward the sergeant.

"My boss just had his gallbladder out."

"He'll be sorry he missed the fun. Who found her, anyway?"

"Cleaning woman."

"Husband? Kids?"

"She lived alone."

"In this?"

"She was a novelist. Orianna Soule."

"Not the one that wrote that bullfight thing?"

"The same."

"My God, maybe it's just as well she's gone. From a literary point of view," he added hastily. "My wife lapped up that book. Kept reading me 'relevant' bits and pieces. I never heard such claptrap."

The two men stood chatting in the pallid sunshine above the mutilated body, neither anxious to attempt to remove Orianna until Prince was secured. Sergeant Putnam was disposed to throw a sheet over her recumbent form, but, not wishing to appear any less hardened than Warren Rupert, he stifled the impulse and kept his eyes on the dog.

Everett returned as far as the porch door to report that Beany and Ted were on their way. Beany, in addition to his periodic police duties, served as a volunteer fireman and the town's dog officer, positions that demanded just enough of his time to make a regular job impossible. Through the new and flawless sheet of glass that had been installed to replace the porch's broken pane, Sergeant Putnam watched Everett, mission accomplished, settle himself comfortably on the wicker settee and experienced his usual burst of irritation at Everett's bland assumption of familiarities.

Beany arrived and stumbled from his truck, stumpy arms overflowing with the tools of his trade. The soiled woolen cap he wore eleven months of the year sat snugly on his custard-colored head, which, with its fringe of hair, resembled nothing so much as a giant sea anemone. He dressed in greasy green chinos and layers of sweatshirts, and reminded Sergeant Putnam of a bear on its hind legs.

Ted, being off-duty and no doubt straight from the garden, was also in casual attire, but Ted's work pants held a crease and his flannel shirt was neatly buttoned at the wrists. He pursed his lips and shook his head at the sight of Orianna, then quite unself-consciously removed his baseball cap and held it over his heart while observing a moment of silent meditation.

Catching sight of the Doberman, his face brightened. He whistled and snapped his fingers, and while Dr. Rupert and Sergeant Putnam frankly retreated and Beany hovered nearby with his noose, the dog rose, trotted straight to Ted, and sniffed his outstretched hand.

"Take aholt of his collar," Beany hissed.

"He's not going anywheres," Ted said, fondling the dog's ears.

71

Sergeant Putnam wished fervently that Ted would stop caressing the animal. He had a terrible vision of Prince casually springing up for a re-run.

"Lemme get this here loop over his head."

"He don't need no loop. He'll come along with me."

"Now, lissen, Ted, this here dog's a killer."

"Treat them right, they don't bite," Ted said firmly, a dictum that did not find hearty endorsement.

The rest of the group relaxed visibly when Prince was muzzled, leashed, and stowed safely within the confines of the truck's cab, through the windshield of which he alertly followed the proceedings. Everett relinquished the shelter of the porch and the ambulance attendants shuffled forward with a stretcher.

"You got somebody to make the positive ident?" Dr. Rupert asked, swinging in behind the wheel of his car.

"You know where she'll be."

Beany and Ted pulled out behind him, en route with Prince to the animal shelter, rather a magniloquent appellation for a couple of sagging wire runs in Beany's backyard where stray dogs were housed until claimed or destroyed. The latter course of action had never appealed to Beany as a legitimate option. Dogs were a casual part of village life, and Beany's charges were rapidly absorbed into the variegated packs of his hunting buddies. Cats just moved in with him.

Ted promised to call Dan Pollock, the veterinarian, to examine Prince as soon as possible. Sergeant Putnam, with Everett, remained at the scene of the tragedy in the hope of augmenting his understanding of it but found nothing helpful. The sole irregularity remained the patch of flattened grass so ominously stained at one end.

In all other respects the garden appeared untouched by the violence done within it. Yellow tulips trembled on their long smooth stems, plum blossoms spiraled gently to earth. Sergeant Putnam could not recall a more peaceable setting for death. No crowds had gathered to murmur and gawk. Orianna's neighbors where either at work or insulated behind acres of clipped lawns and shielding hedges. It was a neighborhood where privacy was the real purchase, where even ambulances slipped discreetly up and down driveways.

Abandoning the garden, the two men proceeded methodically through the house, from kitchen to attic. They found no signs of disturbance or disarrangement. They found, in fact, few signs of occupation as they trod somewhat diffidently through the impressive ground-floor rooms. The color scheme was muted—oyster-white walls, beige carpeting, Early American furnishings, beautifully maintained and artfully authentic in appearance, from the spice cabinet on the kitchen wall to the butter churn on the living room hearth. It was, Sergeant Putnam decided, like walking through a museum. But Everett, springing from one of Hampford's humblest dwellings, found splendor in gloss, whatever the style, and wandered entranced from trestle table to cobbler's bench, every now and then emitting exclamations of envy and pleasure.

In the living room, Sergeant Putnam sorted quickly through the contents of the drawers in a roll-top desk. Orianna's financial records were preserved with care in neatly labeled manila envelopes, which he had neither the time nor the cause to scrutinize closely. In the shallow central drawer, however, amongst a batch of

73

unfiled correspondence, he found a receipt from Home-hearth Kennels for the purchase of Prince.

Upstairs, they wandered through five bedrooms, all furnished to the last Colonial candlestick, and all, to Sergeant Putnam's mind, striking the same sterile note. He looked in vain for an open book, a dirty glass, a depression in a sofa cushion. What had Orianna been doing last night? Had she simply flitted from room to perfect room like some ghostly caretaker? They passed into the master bedroom, where the satin-draped waterbed brought a predictable gasp of delight from Everett, who equated waterbeds with exotic sensual pursuits. One door led to a bathroom, a second to a walk-in closet. Opening the third, they came at last to the nerve center of this dormant dwelling place, a room originally intended perhaps as a dressing room, but now furnished, beneath the single window, with a Formica-topped table holding an electric typewriter, little stacks of index cards, and a neat pile of manu-script. Papers, books, and notebooks were strewn across a second table, twin to the first, that stood against an inside wall. The wastebasket was full, as was an ashtray on the typing table, a sweater hung from the back of the desk chair, and the overhead light was still burning.

While Everett bolted back to the bedroom to fan his fantasies, Sergeant Putnam cursorily examined the manuscript on the table, skimming enough pages to convince himself that Orianna had not been bluffing. She had indeed been engaged in writing, and writing exactly what she had threatened to write. He snapped off the light, shut the door, and left the house with an address book in which he had found the name and telephone number of her literary agent. He might have called any one of the other numbers and found someone closer to Orianna, but the entries were enigmatic, giving him no clues as to relationship.

CHAPTER 10

BEGINNING TO WORRY ABOUT the empty station, Sergeant Putnam collected Verlyn and took her downtown to get her statement. Before they had reached shouting distance of the town hall, however, Verlyn had thrice been observed in the back of the cruiser, and soon the news was out: Verlyn Taggert had been arrested! Old Elmer Armstrong, who had experienced a sense of fearful premonition ever since the cruiser tore past him on its outward journey, hobbled shamelessly in its wake, and under the pretext of taking a rest, settled himself on the wooden stairs that led to the station and turned up his hearing aid for optimum reception.

Sergeant Putnam, having patiently extracted the

substance from Verlyn's dramatic presentation, was continuing his inquiries with the help of Orianna's agent, who, between expressions of genuine shock and distress, acquainted him with Orianna's true name, the name of her ex-husband, and the fact that, as of two years ago, he had still resided in Boston. There was no Krumbaecker, Graham or otherwise, in Orianna's address book.

Sergeant Putnam next placed a call to the Boston police to ask for their help in locating the man, both to inform him of his ex-wife's death and to obtain his assistance in contacting her family. Verlyn, in the meantime, had progressed no farther than the counter, where she was expanding, for Everett's edification, on various sordid details of her morning's experience. Verlyn's normal tone of voice being far from dulcet, such appalling tidbits of information soon began to blast into Elmer's ear that he almost lost his balance.

"By Gorry," he repeated, saliva trickling from the corner of his mouth. "By Gorry. By Gorry."

"What the dickens are you by-gorrying about, Elmer Armstrong?" inquired Sonia Mitchell, who had left her pies to the flies and scurried forth to satisfy her own curiosity. Suddenly, it seemed as though the tree trunks had sprouted people.

"Orianna Soule," Elmer informed them excitedly. "She's been et by her dog."

The gruesome phrases raced around the circle.

"Verlyn fell over the body."

"Gallons of blood."

"All tore up."

"Stark nekid."

Sonia, with an air of self-importance, hurried back to

the bakery to summon Leila Hutchinson, the reporter of Hampford news for the *Mount Pleasant Times*. Leila unplugged her iron, tipped a deaf white cat out of her felt hat, and, armed with pen and notepad, hastened toward the station.

"What the hell's going on out there?" Sergeant Putnam demanded ten minutes later, in the act of dialing Homehearth Kennels. Austin Mead, proprietor and trainer, responded to Sergeant Putnam's inquiry with incredulity. His dogs were renowned throughout New England for the gentleness of their dispositions.

"How can an attack dog be gentle?"

"What do you mean, 'attack dog'?"

"Isn't that what Prince is?"

"He most certainly is not. That's the kind of misconception I've been fighting for years. Did Mrs. Soule tell you she had purchased an attack dog?"

"Not exactly."

"There you are. The correct term, by the way, is 'protection dog.'"

"And he isn't a protection dog?"

"No, he is not."

"Would you call him a watch dog?"

"Only insofar as every dog is a watch dog. He would bark at an intruder, or perhaps emit a little growl or a tweeny snarl, if that's what you mean. But we're talking first and foremost about a companion, Sergeant, a good-natured, loyal, handsome companion."

"I'm not sure good-natured is a term I'd employ right now, Mr. Mead. This particular handsome companion appears to have savagely turned on his owner with fatal results."

"*Appears* is the key word."

79

"I don't know what the hell else ripped her throat out," Sergeant Putnam snapped, losing patience.

A moment's silence ensued. Then, a little more humbly, Austin Mead said, "I think I'd better come up and see what's going on."

"I think you'd better. Prince is at the animal shelter here in Hampford being checked over by a vet. I'd appreciate your dropping by the station after you've seen him."

"Ev," he shouted, simultaneously banging down the receiver, "will you shut up that racket outside."

"Leila's here, Dave," Everett explained as Leila appeared in the doorway shedding wisps of cat fur.

The phone rang. Sergeant Putnam said yes and thank you to a laconic report from the State Police lab to the effect that his piece of granite had borne no fingerprints. Had he really been concerned about a stone?

"Dave, I know you're busy, but somebody's going to file this story and it might as well be me," Leila said hopefully. Most of Leila's news flashes came to rest on the back page of the Mount Pleasant paper under the heading "Items of Local Interest," but every now and then she submitted a vignette of human interest that received two columns and her byline. Many a Hampford refrigerator bore a yellowed clipping of one of Leila's modest triumphs—"Down But Not Out," "One Step at a Time," or the ever popular "Daddy's Boy."

"This is not your usual pet story," Sergeant Putnam said unkindly as he waved her to a chair. Leila had no sooner poised her pencil and assumed an attitude of alert concern than the phone rang again. This time it was Barbara, sounding subdued.

"The most incredible rumors are flying around, Dave. I don't know what to believe. They're saying that Orianna Soule is dead."

"She is. Looks like her dog killed her."

"My God, Dave."

If the story was spreading with gossip's customary speed and inaccuracy, it might be expedient to furnish Leila with the facts and at least attempt to counteract whatever distorted versions were already making the rounds.

Leila scribbled furiously on a notepad adorned with little elves sitting on toadstools, maintaining her professional objectivity except for an occasional "My Lord" or a sorrowful shake of her head that launched more cat hairs into space. They twirled gently downward to moor on the synthetic fabric of her maroon pants suit, the legs of which had hitched up to expose several inches of thin white shin.

"My Lord, Dave, I've reported many a piece of mischief from this town, but this takes the cake. I wouldn't be at all surprised if this wasn't plastered right on page one for all the world to see."

One man's loss is another's gain, thought Sergeant Putnam philosophically, agreeing with her assessment. This might just be a gruesome enough episode to lift Hampford out of obscurity.

He stood up to shoo Leila out and found the station empty. Everett, it seemed, had accompanied Verlyn to the parking lot to add his own attested bits of color to the tale, and clumped grumpily up the stairs when recalled.

"Mrs. Verlyn Eyewitness don't rest her jaw pretty soon, it's gonna fall off. Your phone's ringin', Dave."

"I still have ears, Ev." Sergeant Putnam picked up the receiver.

"Dan Pollock here. I've seen Prince. I don't know exactly what kinds of things you want, but I'll tell you what I found and send you a formal report for the inquest."

"Thanks, Dan."

"He's a hell of a handsome animal, in excellent physical condition, very cooperative. An extremely *intelligent* animal."

Sergeant Putnam waited patiently.

"I found no traces of blood or tissue in the mouth, but you wouldn't expect to after this much time. I did find what look like rope fibers caught between a couple of molars. I've saved them for you. Did she tie him up?"

"I don't know. I'll find out."

"There were splotches of dried blood on both sides of the muzzle and on top of the head. I've taken scrapings and I'll get them to Warren myself for matching. There's always the chance he was chasing chickens."

"You don't believe that, Dan."

"I'm grasping at straws, Dave. He's such a damn fine animal that I hate to think the worst of him. You know, it's rare for a dog to attack alone unless he's hurt or frightened or starving. They usually do damage in packs. I can't imagine what set him off."

"That's what we'd all like to know," Sergeant Putnam told him, before replacing the receiver. "Is there something the matter with me, Ev? I seem to be the only one who's not on the dog's side."

"I ain't," Everett assured him stoutly. "What he done to poor Mrs. Soule is pro'ly the worst thing I ever seen, and I seen some gross sights, you know that,

Dave, like that guy who's arm came off in that crash. You remember that, Dave? And Frankie Bright, that tried out for the Red Sox, when he fell off his dirt bike and skidded on his face?"

"You've made your point, Ev. The next person who calls Prince a splendid animal should have to take a good hard look at Mrs. Soule's throat. You know what I'm thinking? That I ought to call Len before he reads about this in the paper."

Everett agreed. "You don't give him some warnin', he might prolapse when he hears it."

"My thoughts exactly," said Sergeant Putnam craftily, feeling an urge to share the burden of accountability. "It's been almost three days. He ought to be taking some interest in life again."

Catherine, ever vigilant, snatched up the phone on its first ring, but Sergeant Putnam had long practice in wearing down Catherine. Soon, Len's familiar irascible tones were floating over the wire.

"How are you, Len?"

"Worse than I was two minutes ago. You're either wasting time or you've got yourself in trouble. Which is it?"

"Now, Len, we've had an accident in town, that's all, but it's going to make the papers and I want you to know about it before it does."

"What?" the chief roared, exploding with enough power to blast himself off the bed. Instantly, Catherine started hushing and fussing. "I *am* calm. Do *not* call the nurse. Go ahead, Dave. I'm calm."

Sergeant Putnam deftly summarized the happenings of the past ten days, culminating with Orianna's death.

Len grunted periodically as the story unfolded. At

83

the end, he muttered, "Jesus Christ, that's horrible," but excitement sharpened his outrage. "Tell me what you've done."

Sergeant Putnam ticked off a list item by item.

"Sounds like you covered everything," the chief conceded grudgingly. "So what's the problem?"

"Who said there was any problem?"

"Don't play cute with me, Dave. I know you, remember?"

"It's a very minor point, Len. It's just that when we went into the house this morning we found all the lights off except the one in Orianna's workroom. Now, something brought her downstairs. Say she turned on the hall light at the top of the stairs; she must have turned it off again at the bottom of the stairs. She could have crossed the living room by the light from the porch. There's a spotlight over the side porch door and another on the back of the house that illuminates about thirty feet of lawn, including the spot where she was found. But the porch lights weren't on this morning. Would she cross a pitch-dark living room and a pitch-dark porch without turning on a light? Would she go outside to investigate a noise, or let out Prince, or let in Prince, without a light? I just don't know. It seems she did, I mean she must have, but it kind of bothers me."

"Oh, Dave, if I had a dollar for every time I've heard those words, I could retire tomorrow. You go right ahead and cogitate about porch lights all you want—*on your own time*. Meanwhile, I expect that department to run as smoothly as a pig on a greased rail. Give me a call when you've seen the dog man. Keep me posted on everything. I'm bored out of my skull, Dave. Call me every five minutes if you want to. Who's that yelling?"

84

"That's Ev, Len. He's saying hello and he's glad you're better."

"You got Ted there, too?"

"Ted is with the dog."

"Of course Ted is with the dog. I'd forgotten the realities of my workplace. I'm telling you, Dave, even our psychic garbageman is going to look good to me, that's how desperate I've become."

CHAPTER 11

LEILA, IN DEPARTING, HAD, like a Pied Piper, swept the spectators with her, except for Bea Lambert, who, had with her usual perverse, or uncanny, prescience, arrived just in time for Act II, trotting expectantly into the room behind Ted and Austin Mead. The owner of Homehearth Kennels was a shaken man. His visit to Prince, specifically the bloody stigmata on the dog's muzzle, had shocked him into a brutal awareness of the facts. Ted steered him gently to the chair in front of Sergeant Putnam's desk and assumed a position beside it as though supporting the forces of dogdom. Bea and Everett stared quite unabashedly, Bea in fascination and Everett with a repulsive rustic revulsion toward anything unusual, a repugnance Sergeant Putnam hoped to God would not find oral expression.

Still, he was forced to acknowledge his own surprise. Somehow one pictured dog trainers as weathered and tweedy. Austin Mead looked far too elegant to heft a bag of dog chow. He possessed the disconcerting combination of a youthful body and an aging face; beneath the out-of-season tan, one could see the faint crow's-feet and incipient pouches. His styled blond hair and cream-colored flannel slacks, pale-green silk shirt, and forest-green lambswool pullover rendered him as foreign to the streets of Hampford as a Martian.

"Excuse me, Captain," said Austin Mead, and, producing a clean white silk handkerchief, he patted the sweat from his upper lip while the gallery viewers looked on goggle-eyed. Sergeant Putnam could only hope, by treating their presence casually, to lull his visitor into the misconception that old ladies and cretinous patrolmen were standard witnesses to his interviews.

"I am just assimilating the horror of the situation," Austin Mead said.

"Prince licked his hand," Ted reported dolefully.

"He was happy to see me, poor fellow. I simply *cannot* understand it."

"She'd had him only a few days. Could that have made a difference?" Sergeant Putnam asked.

"I don't know why it would. Our dogs work with a variety of handlers. Mrs. Soule seemed very competent. I felt they were an excellent match."

"Did she tell you why she chose a Doberman?"

"She said she had always admired them."

88

"She didn't tell you she'd been a victim of vandalism? Didn't say she was looking for protection?"

"No, she did not. I don't see that it matters, in any case. Most dogs play a double role. Even a Pekinese can set up a racket in the advent of a prowler."

A yippy little racket, thought Sergeant Putnam, that wouldn't fool a cat, much less a prowler, but he abandoned his attempt to clarify Orianna's motives. Whatever her knowledge of Prince's nature, she had represented him to the town as a vicious attack dog.

"I suppose," Austin Mead ventured with some distaste, "that the media are going to have a field day with this, aren't they? Is it preposterous to ask that the identity of the kennel remain our little secret? It's not what you're thinking," he added quickly, raising a hand as though to forestall criticism. "I am not eschewing responsibility."

Not in front of me, you ain't, a scandalized Everett agreed silently. Whatever it was, it sounded obscene.

"After all, it's of the utmost importance to me to discover the cause of the dog's aberrant behavior. I truly believe this incident is a once-in-a-lifetime occurrence—a fluke, if you will—and to create a wave of hysteria that might very well deprive me of the source of my livelihood would be quite unfair to both myself and my dogs. If facts should prove otherwise—if I am indeed raising a kennel full of killers—I give you my word, I shall personally destroy each and every animal."

The pathos of this pledge brought moisture to Ted's eyes, but Sergeant Putnam, recalling Orianna's wounds, remained as cold as an iceberg.

"I don't think anything as drastic as that will be

necessary, Mr. Mead. We're certainly not out to crucify you. But neither can we minimize the seriousness of the situation."

"Oh, my God, no," Austin Mead agreed, rising and slipping a small tanned hand into Sergeant Putnam's freckled paw. "The seriousness is weighing on me like a stone. I feel as though I shall never be happy again."

"Come now, sir," Ted said comfortingly, escorting him toward the door. "It's always darkest before the dawn."

Ted had a great stock of such banalities upon which to draw in time of need. "It never rains but it pours," he would proclaim solemnly at an appropriate moment. "A stitch in time saves nine." "Waste not, want not." He would deliver these old saws with all the reverence customarily accorded a new and marvelous truth, and would no more have questioned their validity than he would have dipped the American flag to the ground.

Now, having assured Austin Mead that every cloud has a silver lining, he shut the screen door behind him and approached Sergeant Putnam's desk.

"Here, Dave, I almost forgot. These are the rope fibers that were caught in Prince's teeth. Dan sent them over."

Sergeant Putnam, once more lifting the telephone receiver, stretched out his free hand for the envelope. The caller was Graham Krumbaecker, sounding wary, as if he suspected the Hampford police of conspiring with Orianna to make a fool of him. Sergeant Putnam satisfied him that Orianna was not playing jokes, that she was well and truly dead.

"Did she leave a will?" demanded Krumbaecker, which struck Sergeant Putnam as a crass inquiry coming from an ex-husband, particularly in view of the fact that their divorce, according to Orianna, had been notoriously unamiable.

"I have no idea. You'll have to call her lawyer. Do you think you could come out here to make a formal identification? How about funeral arrangements?"

"I guess I'll have to do it all," Krumbaecker said sourly.

"She has no family?"

"Who knows?"

"You mean she never mentioned anyone?"

"She said there had been an 'estrangement.' That's all she said and all she ever would say. I don't even know what part of the country she came from. Not that I cared. I didn't marry her family, after all. If she didn't load me with a lot of in-laws, I certainly wasn't going to push her into doing so. No one pushed her into anything, anyway. I hear she has quite a house in Hampford. What's going to happen to that?"

"Mr. Krumbaecker, you'll have to deal with her lawyer. Are you coming out here or aren't you?"

"What's her lawyer's name?"

Sergeant Putnam hung up rather sharply and sent Everett to the drugstore for sandwiches and coffee.

Bea said, "I take it her ex is not grieving."

"The sad thing, Bea, is that nobody is grieving. He'll come only because he thinks there's something in it for him."

"Maybe he deserves something," Bea said, sidling around the counter and into the chair vacated by Austin Mead. "Did you see that fellow's shoes? I think they were made of dog skin."

"They never were," Ted said, shocked, and Sergeant Putnam caught the gleam in Bea's eye.

"When I think of a dog breeder," said Bea, "I think of a real dog breeder. I think of Myrtle Wing. I can see her now in her rubber boots and that man's overcoat with the buttons gone, her gray hair sticking up every which way. I think she cut it with dog clippers. How she cussed out those animals. 'By God, sir, you *will* sit.'"

"It's a wonder it wasn't *her* throat that was torn out," Ted agreed with a chuckle. "Say, Bea, do you think she really ate Milk Bones with her tea?"

"No, she balanced them on her nose," snapped Sergeant Putnam. "I hate to inhibit this stream of reminiscences, but I have work to do."

"What work?" Bea asked mildly, regarding him with her faded blue eyes. "What do you have to do that you haven't done?"

What *did* he have to do? Warren Rupert would fill out the death certificate and supply medical evidence for the inquest at which Austin Mead was primed to appear, the dog was secured and had been examined, Orianna's next of kin informed, the press and Len supplied with the facts, and the Chapel Road house locked up, awaiting its disposition. Surely, he'd covered all the bases.

Yet he remained restive. He surveyed with distaste Everett's stack of oozing egg salad sandwiches and the carton of Styrofoam coffee cups. What the hell kind of station was it anyway, he thought irritably, in which the senior patrolman, in flannel shirt and with manure on his boots, placidly exchanged snippets of scandal with an elderly citizen who wandered in and out as though the room were her backyard? At that moment, Everett sloshed coffee on his trousers and his casual snicker at yet another stain made Sergeant Putnam want to scream.

"I'm going out," he said abruptly, ignoring their startled faces. It was cruel, really, like leaving a trio of house pets, but he hardened his heart, clapped on his cap, and left in an aura of mystery.

The morning's mild promise had ripened into a full-blown spring day drenched with sparkling sunshine, the kind of day that made winter seem like a delusion. He rolled down the front windows of the cruiser and pulled into Main Street, fighting a momentary inclination to go completely wild and spend the afternoon at Turtle Pond, attempting to recapture the childhood magic of dabbling in muddy water and green slime through long tranquil hours. He supposed there were seacoast inhabitants whose memories revived with a whiff of salt air or the sight of a periwinkle, but his spring had been polliwogs and skunk cabbage.

Without ever having settled on a plan of action, he found himself once again pulling into Orianna's driveway. The tulips greeted him benignly. Bees were boring into the hyacinths beside the porch steps, tapping each tiny star for its nectar. He unlocked the door and entered. The house, even in so short a time, had acquired the stale odor of a closed-up building. Stifling an urge to throw open windows, he poked around in the kitchen, found a cup, a plate, and some silverware in the dishwasher, reminded himself to ask Verlyn to clean out the refrigerator, and climbed the steps to Orianna's workroom, to which, he realized, he had been heading all along.

Standing by the table, he began to leaf through the manuscript, reading one page and then another. After a while, he sat down. She hadn't done that much, about thirty pages in all, and the style, even to his untutored ear, struck him as embarrassingly breathless. But, by God, here were the Pulhams and the Coffins and half a dozen other recognizable figures. Lost in thought, he restacked the sheets of manuscript. Gathering up the index cards spread out on the table, he shoved them into his jacket pocket and confiscated a second pile from the table against the wall. Then, slipping the manuscript into a manila envelope, he took that, too, experiencing a momentary conviction of the appropriateness of his action, though quite unable to explain why.

When Sergeant Putnam arrived back at the station, he discovered that Ted had gone home, changed into his uniform, and returned to lend his gracious support, all on overtime. Bea, in the meantime, had hastened to her Friendly Wheel meeting, where tongues would flash faster than needles as the good ladies assembled their layettes. Everett, for lack of anything better to do, was dispatched to the post office with the day's mail and the resignation, on Sergeant Putnam's part, to a slow return. Routine matters drifted in, easing out the morning's crisis, and by four-thirty he was amenable to Ted's suggestion that he make it an early afternoon.

"You'll start growing moss if you stay here much longer. I can always call if something comes up. An ounce of prevention—"

"Right, Ted."

He was halfway to the door when the telephone rang.

"I thought you were going to call me," Chief Henderson said plaintively.

"Nothing to report, Len. We had the dog's breeder here, a fellow named Austin Mead from the Home-hearth Kennels. Very shaken up, naturally, but he had no explanation for Prince's behavior. None of his dogs has ever done anything like this before."

"He wouldn't be in business if they had," Len said tartly. "I've been thinking about those lights, Dave. You know, if she thought there was someone in the yard, she might have come down in the dark and let the dog out to surprise him."

"That's true, Len."

"And then if Prince didn't come when she called, she might have gone out to look for him, and the dog might have mistaken *her* for the prowler. That's how I see it, anyway."

"Yeah, it makes sense. I kind of wonder about those rope fibers though."

"Rope fibers?"

"That were caught between a couple of the dog's teeth. Dan Pollock found them and gave them to me, and I've sent them over to the lab. I looked around Orianna's house this afternoon and I couldn't find a trace of any rope, so I called Tim Twomey, the kid who's been working up there, and he said the dog was never tied with rope, or anything else for that matter. When he took him walking, he used a leather leash with a choke collar."

"There's a simple explanation, Dave. How long did you say she'd had the dog?"

"Three or four days."

"So he got those fibers between his teeth before she bought him. In the kennel. I mean, how often does anyone check a dog's teeth?"

"That's true. I'm sure you're right, Len."

Sergeant Putnam didn't tell him he was going home—Chief Henderson liked to picture him on duty twenty-four hours a day—but he amazed and delighted Barbara with his unexpected emancipation, and after he had changed out of his uniform into a T-shirt and jeans, they took a couple of bottles of beer out to the redwood lounges in the backyard. Jennifer was playing next door; the boys were about their own business.

"I'd forgotten I had a home," Sergeant Putnam said, stretching contentedly beneath the still-warm sun. And he described for Barbara the day's events in direct contravention of Len's oft-stated policy of zipping lips at the station door. Of course, Len's viewpoint had been warped by personal circumstances. Sergeant Putnam would have zipped up, too, tighter than a clam, if he had been going home to Catherine.

"I don't see how else it could have happened," Barbara said thoughtfully after her husband had finished. "It's just one of those horrible accidents that makes us widen life's stakes, one more thing to wake me up in a sweat in the middle of the night."

Not until supper was over did Sergeant Putnam remember Orianna's manuscript. Barbara, having put Jenny to bed, came downstairs to find him at the kitchen table sorting stacks of index cards.

"She managed to mention five families in thirty pages," he said. "I'm just wondering how many more she had in mind."

Barbara sat down beside him, skimmed the manuscript, poked through the cards, and soon became so engrossed that Sergeant Putnam, sleepily headed for bed, said good night three time before she replied.

CHAPTER 12

NEITHER COLD TABLETS, NOSE drops, nor Vicks Vaporub had the salubrious effect on Harley Bower as did Vesta's announcement of Orianna's death.

"What a terrible thing," Harley said, rising from his bed.

Albert scorned even a pretense of regret. "God moves in mysterious ways," said Albert, complacently.

Harley spent the afternoon with his stamp collection, sitting peacefully in the spring sunshine at the little cherry table by the bay window in the dining room, and Vesta made meringues for supper, a dessert that always signified a special occasion in the Bower household.

Across town, at the Coffins' gray-shingled domicile,

the reaction was somewhat more variant. For Grandma and Wilma, Orianna's death was a horrible, shocking accident that did not, as far as they knew, touch them personally.

"Life is hard on the wimmen," Grandma observed, an opinion she was prone to supply with very little encouragement. Since she could always match or surpass any present event with something equal or worse from the past, the uniqueness of Orianna's demise was soon eclipsed by rambling remembrances of a bullgoring that had similarly appalled the town in 'ought-eight or 'ought-nine.

Scott's arrival at four o'clock refocused attention on the current tragedy. He and Terry had heard the news at school, where it had momentarily taken precedence over the everyday concerns of the adolescent community—who was writing the swear words on the walls of the girls' second-floor lavatory and the fact that Lendell Ashhouse was going to sue Mr. Keene for slamming him against the blackboard ("He coulda busted my friggin' skull," declared the young victim).

Scott, naturally, was thinking of his father coming home from a day with his potato chips, coming home to the news that his secret was safe. He was happy for his dad and frankly relieved on his own behalf. He saw no sense, as matters now stood, in relating any of these conjectures to Robyn. In fact, it was his honest conviction that his father had escalated the whole thing out of perspective, but whether his fear had a real or imagined source, the effect was the same, and Scott rejoiced at the thought of his father's deliverance from it.

Terry, who was waiting in the garage, standing

patiently among the rakes and spades, got to him first. Since Gil Coffin was habituated to seeing Terry materialize from behind garden hoses and hedges, he swung out of the car with a cheery greeting.

"Hi, there, Terry boy."

Terry came up very close to his father and, frowning into his face, said, "Bad news, Dad. Mrs. Soule got killed by her dog."

"What?"

"Bad news, Dad. Mrs. Soule got killed by her dog."

"Are you sure? Who said so?" Gilbert Coffin ran for the house at a pace that left Terry jogging to catch up. "What's all this about Mrs. Soule?" he shouted, barging in upon the women.

Meanwhile, up in Dogtown, Merlin Stroud was sitting at his kitchen table with a can of beer, surrounded by his wife Juanita, three of their seven children, his brother-in-law, two aunts, an uncle, and assorted cousins. The room bulged with Strouds and large gleaming appliances: a refrigerator-freezer, an electric stove, a washing machine and dryer. Merlin had done well for a Dogtown boy.

"You going back on the committe now, Merl?" asked his brother-in-law, Baily.

"Sure, I am. It was only her that was causing the problems. She had it in for us."

Baily said, "You know what I think? I think she was one of us. I think somewheres along the line there was some Native American blood and she was ashamed of it."

"She had the hair," Juanita agreed.

"She was no Wompanaki," Merlin stated flatly.

"Oh, no, probably Bagawump."

And they all shared a good laugh.

Until the inquest a week later, Orianna's death remained the town's obsession. Reverend Mayflower took as his text on Sunday "Indeed many dogs surround me," and built upon these lines a maundering discourse on the alarming unpredictability of household pets. A stranger might be forgiven the assumption of symbolism, might satisfactorily equate Reverend Mayflower's dogs, cats, and bunnies with our untamed impulses or the forces of evil, but Hampfordites knew better than to complicate the address with subtle allusions. They knew that when Reverend Mayflower said, "Don't turn your back on your cat," he meant exactly that.

Little bits of information trickled in that were helpful in reconstructing Orianna's last hours but did little to illuminate them. Phyllis McCabe, who lived on Spruce Ridge and was about the closest Orianna had come to a friend in Hampford, called Sergeant Putnam on Wednesday morning to say that she had spoken to Orianna on the phone about half-past eight Monday night.

"How did she sound?"

"What do you mean, how did she sound?"

"Did she sound nervous or distracted? We think she might have heard something that caused her to go outside."

"Oh, I see. It's funny, but I never wondered why she went out. She did say just before she hung up that she had to let the dog out, but she didn't mention going out herself. She certainly didn't sound alarmed. In fact, quite the opposite. She'd had a visitor just before I called—a Mr. X, was how she put it. Someone who came to see her about the book."

"He threatened her?" Sergeant Putnam asked quickly.

"I don't know if he threatened, bribed, or begged her, but she certainly wasn't frightened. She said the longer she lived, the more ridiculous men appeared to her."

Sergeant Putnam could easily believe those had been Orianna's words. They had the ring of authenticity.

The inquest on Wednesday morning returned the expected verdict of accidental death. Dr. Rupert stated unequivocally that Orianna had died of dog bites. Moreover, the blood on Prince's muzzle matched Orianna's B-positive blood type. Sergeant Putnam was called upon to describe the scene as he had found it, and Verlyn had her brief moment in the spotlight. Austin Mead and Dan Pollock attempted to balance the general tone of the hearing by presenting the dog as less than satanic, but their defense appeared perverted in the face of Dr. Rupert's gruesome photographs. In a separate judgment, Prince was ordered destroyed and Homehearth Kennels closed for a year.

"He got off easy at that," Chief Henderson said when Sergeant Putnam reported the decision. "They could have shut him down for good. He better feed those pups less red meat."

Len had come home, as he'd predicted he would, on the Thursday following Orianna's death, but on doctor's orders, and with Catherine as warden, had immediately been put under house arrest for the weekend. Monday he'd staged a revolt, arriving at the station with a grim-faced Catherine behind the wheel for the express purpose of dispatching Sergeant Putnam homeward. Tuesday he'd not only accelerated his pace to an eight-hour day but had announced his intention of assuming his rightful place on the pageant committee. The previous week's meeting had been cancelled in deference to Orianna's mishap, and the need for renewed activity was paramount, since the group had not yet produced a working script, let alone begun the tasks of casting and rehearsing. Sergeant Putnam, with a sigh of relief, had relinquished his position as alternate and was looking forward to a quiet evening at home.

Chief Henderson had managed, in just three days' time, to ruck up the office rug, spill books out of his bookcase, cover his desktop with manila folders, and the folders with flakes of tobacco. Styrofoam mugs of cold coffee were strategically located over the surface of the desk, and wrappers of Twinkies and Yodels, screwed up and flipped in the direction of the wastebasket, littered the rug. The air was fuzzy with pipe smoke, the windows firmly sealed. Len was back in the seat of power, seemingly not one whit diminished by the ordeal of surgery. His small, spare frame was as straight as ever, his eyes as bright a blue, his humor as caustic. He did not mention his absence, the embarrassement of physical weakness being best forgotten as quickly as possible. Neither did a word of praise, however faint, pass his thin lips. The chief did not believe in "spoiling" his staff.

Now, contemplating Sergeant Putnam's long face, he said, "Does this mean what I think it means? That the Commonwealth of Massachusetts is satisfied with the verdict but Sergeant David Putnam is not?"

"Nobody brought up the question of the lights."

"Why the hell should they have? The answer is self-evident."

"Then explain the rope fibers. Austin Mead said the dog was never tied at the kennel. He was as shocked at the suggestion as if I had accused him of viviscetion. Orianna didn't tie him up, either. There's not a scrap of rope at her house heavier than garden twine, certainly no nylon cord, and the State Police lab said the fibers came from nylon cord."

"So didn't he ever go out on his own? Certainly he did. She told Phyllis McCabe that she had to *let* Prince out, not *take* him out. How do we know how many times a day she did that?"

"Never, when Tim was there."

"He wasn't there first thing in the morning or last thing at night. That's when dogs go out, Dave. Soon as I get up, I push Peppy out the door and he makes his little circuit around the yard and waddles in again. Same thing before I go to bed. Now Prince, being a young dog, maybe he roamed around a bit, picked up a stick here, a piece of rope there. What else are you suggesting? If Warren Rupert says she died of dog bites, then she died of dog bites."

"But, Len—"

"Finished, over, done, that's it. I'm a man of incredible patience, but I've indulged you long enough. Have you checked the house this morning?"

"I'm going to now."

Orianna had died without a will, which meant still another headache for the Hampford Police Department. Until her estate was settled, her property was their responsibility. "There's nothing I hate more than an empty building," Chief Henderson had grumbled when the news reached him, "especially this one, with the curiosity factor and all those nice things to tempt the temptable. I suppose Krumbaecker thinks they belong to him."

In the week since the accident, they had coined a number of descriptive titles for Orianna's ex-husband, who'd become a definite nuisance. Having taken charge of the funeral arrangements, the whereabouts of her family having died with her, he seemed to feel this restored to him certain conjugal rights and had retained a local lawyer to represent his claims. Each day brought at least one call from the lawyer, or from Graham himself, who had begun to sniff around for something publishable, having realized the impetus that the manner of her death would give to new work.

"I can only tell you what I've already told her agent," Sergeant Putnam had said. "There isn't any new book. Just a few notes."

"Then get me the notes," Graham replied. "I can't go into the house. You can. It would be to your advantage."

"Goodness, I can't do that," Sergeant Putnam said primly, thinking guiltily of the index cards spread across his kitchen table. "Nothing can be released until we find out to whom her things belong."

In the meantime, watching over Orianna's estate translated into demands on everyone's time. Sergeant Putnam swung up Chapel Road for his morning check still smarting from Len's dismissal, although he sympathized with his chief's viewpoint. He himself felt that he was often inordinately obdurant, but he had the kind of mind that moves doggedly from point to point in a straight line, and which, when it meets with obstructions, has to stop and worry each one through, persistent rather than intuitive. If he were to remain true to his own nature, he had no choice other than to peck away, undercover if need be, until all the vexing details, however trivial or irrelevant, were explained to his own satisfaction.

If he could find Orianna's mysterious Mr. X, he thought as he unlocked her porch door, he might at least get some partial answers to his questions. Easier said than done, of course. He knew nothing about her nocturnal visitor except his sex, and while that fact disqualified half the population of Hampford, it left the other half a wide-open field. If Mr. X had slunk across the backyard, his detection was hopeless, but if he had come by car, there was a remote chance that someone had seen him enter or leave Orianna's driveway. Sergeant Putnam had previously been assured by her neighbors that they had seen or heard nothing unusual on the night of Orianna's death, but he was seeking the trivial this time, not the dramatic. Sometimes a slightly different emphasis in a subsequent interview brought forth new information.

CHAPTER
13

Hᴉꜱ ʜᴏᴘᴇꜱ, ᴀᴅᴍɪᴛᴛᴇᴅʟʏ ꜰʀᴀɪʟ, met with little encouragement at the Russells'. Winifred was as friendly and cooperative as a body could be, but the fact remained that she and Rusty had been snug and oblivious within their habitation throughout the evening in question. She seemed so apologetic for the placidity of their lives, and so anxious to be of help, that Sergeant Putnam withdrew before she perjured herself.

The Billings, neighbors on the other side, were both at work; he would have to catch them in the evening. Of the dwelling across the road he had no expectations, since it seemed the least promising of the three immediate possibilities. Orianna's house wasn't even visible from the Keysons', and he walked up to the door convinced that he would have to extend his inquiries farther up and down the street.

His knock produced a jiggling of the latch and a shrill little voice that issued an unintelligible command. Then a stronger hand took over and Alison Keyson opened the door with a baby girl balanced on her hip and towheaded Peter grinning at her knee. Alison was the youngest daughter of Clint Pearson, Hampford's general practitioner. Her husband, Parker Keyson, was embarked on a successful career as a financial analyst for the Mount Pleasant branch of a national firm of investment consultants. It was general knowledge, however, that the young couple could not have afforded Chapel Road without the generosity of Parker's dad, who had the local monopoly on cemetery monuments.

The omniscience of a small-town policeman was an aspect of Sergeant Putnam's work that periodically oppressed him. How he yearned to encounter on the other side of the threshold, just once, a total stranger, someone alien in every sense of the word, an image to be defined through his own skill and effort. Conjecture became meaningless when the sum total was familiar, when he'd watched, for example, Alison progress from chubby kindergartner to wife and mother, when he remembered the name of her childhood doggie and knew that the scar on her left leg was the result of a fall from her bike onto a broken soda bottle.

Fortunately, Alison was unaware that the sight of her had ignited his restive spirit. She greeted him cheerfully and Peter was soon hanging onto his legs.

"He's grown a foot."

"They're both big," Alison said with the complacency of the young and untested. "What can I do for you, Dave? You silly thing."

"What?" he asked, startled, and then realized she was speaking to the baby, who had shyly hidden her face against her mother's neck.

"I'm still looking into Mrs. Soule's death, Alison, tying up the loose ends, you might say. I know you told me you didn't hear or see anything unusual, and I'm sure you didn't, but I'd like you to think back to that evening again. She had a visitor before she died and I'm hoping that someone caught sight of him coming or going."

"You mean Johnny Sparhawk?"

Sergeant Putnam blinked. It couldn't be *that* easy. "You saw Johnny over there?"

"Parker did. We'd gone to the Bests' for cocktails— that's Parker's boss. They were entertaining a VIP from Bangor. Anyway, we got back here about eight-fifteen and Parker drove Mrs. Burleigh home. As he was turning into our driveway he saw a blue Ford pickup coming through the gates of Mrs. Soule's driveway. He knew it was Johnny because of the license plate. When Parker came in he said it appeared that Mrs. Soule had a new admirer, and we laughed about it. I mean, Johnny is *so* awful."

"You didn't mention this last week."

"I didn't even think of it. She had people coming and going, just like we all do. If it hadn't been Johnny, we'd never have given it a thought. I'm sorry if I should have said something and didn't."

Sergeant Putnam reassured her that she had been

most helpful, coaxed a smile from baby Megan, let Peter try on his cap, and went on his way completely cured of his longing for urban anonymity. What big-city Parker would have noticed a single, undistinguished Ford pickup, would have remembered, surrounded by more subtle and sophisticated vanity plates, the legend MACHO 1, or even more improbably, have known as quickly as his own brother's name, the identity of MACHO?

Johnny Sparhawk, in his job as lineman for the telephone company, started his workday early and got home by four o'clock. He was a versatile fellow, was Johnny. He hunted for his meat and fished for his fish, raised his vegetables in a flourishing garden, over-hauled his own truck, car, and snowmobile, and did all the maintenance work on his house. A few years younger than Sergeant Putnam, he carried an extra fifty pounds concentrated in a belly of such magnifi-cence that it refused to be restrained by ordinary garments and flowed over his belt and burst through his shirts with a primitive force that was awesome. Johnny was living with his third wife and had sired, through carelessness, half a dozen children at whose juvenile level he interacted, when visiting or being visited, making extravagant promises when expansive and retaliating when hurt.

Sergeant Putnam, having filled the day with routine matters, drove out to Johnny's house on Turtle Pond at quarter past four and found Johnny in his Madewell work clothes splitting firewood in the yard. Johnny had a predilection for mountain-man gear: greasy vests, union suits, and knee boots. Today he had wound a purple bandana around his head and a gold earring gleamed through his red beard. The house was a modest ranch to which he'd added two rooms and a patio. It backed onto seven or eight acres of land that sloped down to the shore.

Johnny swung up his maul in greeting, holding it for a long moment at arm's length, not with the intention of impressing Sergeant Putnam, but simply because his whole day was a series of tests of strength, the successful execution of which served as the source of his self-esteem. Hounds sprawled over the doorstep or lay in the shade of the truck, a beagle was busy quartering the field that stretched to the pond, and an overweight golden retriever heaved herself to her feet, and tail waving, waddled stiff-legged to Sergeant Putnam's side and gently took his hand in her mouth.

"Goddamn friendliest dogs in the world," Johnny said fondly, while Sergeant Putnam pried open the retriever's jaws and wiped the slobber off his hand with a handkerchief. "What can I do for you, Dave? How about a beer?"

"That would go down nicely."

Johnny reached into the cab of his truck, hauled out a Styrofoam cooler, and extracted two cans of Budwieser.

"Your kids want a pup? I got six of the cutest. Mixed breed, no pedigree, but good pets."

"No thanks, I—"

"You guys like radishes? Why the hell do I plant so many radishes?"

"Johnny, the beer will do me fine."

"So how are you anyways, Dave? I haven't seen you for a coon's age."

"Everything's fine, Johnny. I—"

"Still catchin' the bad guys? I thoughta joinin' the force, but the pay sucks."

"Johnny, I'm piecing together Mrs. Soule's last night, trying to get a picture of it in my mind. I understand you were up to her house the evening she died."

"Yeah, I was. I dunno your source of info, but it don't matter. There was nothin' secret about my visit. I went up to see her and I'll tell you why. She was writin' this book about the old days, right, and I says to myself, if she's usin' my name and the story of my family, then she owes me somethin', right?"

"You asked her for money?"

"That's right. For the use of my name and family history."

"What did she say?"

"Said she didn't have to pay me nothin', it was all in books that was available to anyone. 'Public knowledge,' I think that's what she said. I said maybe I'd check with a lawyer about that and she said, don't bother, she'd already checked with *her* lawyer. So then I says, what about somethin' good that ain't in any book anywheres. She says, about your family? I says, mine or any other. What if I was to act as consultant, like, and you could pay by the piece. Because, Jesus H. Christ, Dave, we got enough dirt in our family alone, I wouldn'ta had to make up nothin', or not much anyways. She'd be gettin' value for her money."

"You were going to sell family secrets?"

"If they was worth anything. You want another beer?"

"No thanks, I'm still working on this one."

"That goddamn choppin' gives me a thirst," Johnny said, dragging out his cooler.

"Anyways, she turned me down, but that don't mean nothin' with a dame. They always say no when they mean yes. I woulda had her in the palm of my hand," he continued sadly, "but she went and died. That really shook me up, you know, her goin' right after we had our chat."

"Where did this chat take place?"

"On her porch, Dave, her glass porch that got the rock through the window."

"Lights were on?"

"Goddamn place was lit up like a prison yard—garage light, porch lights. Inside, the room to the right downstairs—I think it musta been the livin' room. She came outa that room when I knocked and I could hear a TV goin' in there. Then she turned on a light on the porch."

"How about upstairs?"

"Dark."

"You're sure?"

"Dark upstairs."

"Where was the dog?"

"He was sittin' right next to her chair."

"I mean when you knocked on the door."

"Oh. When I knocked he come out of the kitchen and looked at me through the glass."

"He didn't bark?"

"Not a peep. Them killer dogs don't bark. Quiet and deadly, that's how they're trained."

"You weren't afraid to go in there with this killer dog at the door?"

"Naw, Dave, I've took every self-defense course goin'. The dog sensed my power. He backed right down."

"Then you two had your little chat?"

"That's right. We talked fifteen, twenty minutes, just enough to lay the groundwork, like. A lot is done without words, Dave, if you know what I mean. She wasn't a bad-lookin' chick for her age," he added reminiscently. "I think I coulda had her."

Sure you could've, Johnny.

"Then I got the news how she died. That was an awful thing the way she went. I had a shepherd turned on me once. I hadda break his neck. But she was helpless, poor thing." In the grip of some kind of emotion, he crushed the empty beer can between his beefy hands.

"So you left about when, Johnny? Eight-thirty?"

"About eight-thirty. I was on my way to Barney's, over to Mount Pleasant."

"You mean the bar and grill on Commerce Street?"

"Yeah. There's a nice bunch of guys there, Dave. They ain't had it easy, you know. We all got our money troubles. Anyways, to make a long story short, my second wife, Wynette, is screwin' me for more child support, that's one thing. You know how it is. I got to thinkin' on the way home that I'd just give Mrs. Soule a ring and get things settled."

It required little imagination to picture Johnny full of beer and self-pity and grandiose schemes.

"So I give her a ring, maybe ten, ten-fifteen, say ten-fifteen, and she cut me short. 'I can't talk now,' she says, and you know what that means."

"Do I?"

"It means she had a guy there."

"Did you hear him?"

"I didn't have to hear him. When a dame says she

can't talk now in that tone of voice, it means only one thing. Well, I understand that, see, and I hung right up. I'll call tomorrow, I says to myself, but tomorrow was too late."

"When you left Mrs. Soule's, Johnny, were the same lights on as when you came?"

"Lights, lights, these lights seem to be pryin' on your mind, Dave. Don't worry, I won't ask why. But I can tell you that the lights was on, livin' room, porch, and outside."

"And the dog stayed in?"

"The dog was in."

"Well, thanks a lot, Johnny."

"You're surely welcome. I ain't askin' what you're after, Dave, but any help I can give you, I'm glad to do it. I know just about everything that goes on in this town."

"I'll remember that."

Sergeant Putnam was escorted to the cruiser by the retriever, who diligently carried out her duties as hostess and saw him off with much tail thumping and a little heavy breathing. God's gift to women had gathered up the battered tin plates and bowls that lay scattered around the yard and was wading toward the house through a milling pack of dogs. There appeared to be no one else at home. Was it possible that wife number three had, like her predecessors, pulled her scattered female wits together and walked out?

CHAPTER 14

SERGEANT PUTNAM DECLINED TO mention his extracurricular activities to Chief Henderson, there being no sane reason to do so. Instead, Barbara, after supper, became his captive audience, and while he loaded the dishwasher and she swept the floor, he described his clandestine undertakings.

"You see what I mean, hon? Here's Orianna watching TV in the living room, and all the outside lights are on. Johnny comes to the door, she turns on yet another light, on the porch, and invites him in. All perfectly normal, right?"

"Except for letting Johnny in. I wouldn't get near him if he was in a cage," said Barbara.

"Maybe she felt safe with the dog. For whatever reasons, she did let him in and they sat and talked for about twenty minutes, after which he left her with the dog inside and the lights on. A few minutes later she was chatting to Phyllis, and she mentioned Johnny's visit. At the end of the call she said, 'I have to let Prince out, he's whining at the door.' Which meant, if Prince was at the door, that she was still downstairs. There's a phone in the kitchen. Then she must have gone upstairs to write, because the light was on in her workroom the next morning, and it hadn't been on when Johnny came or left. At ten-fifteen he called her and got the impression that someone was with her. And shortly thereafter she was outside the house, dead, and all the downstairs lights were off. Does that make sense?"

"People do strange things, love."

"That's what Len said."

"Well, he's right. *I* would not go out into a dark yard after someone had thrown a rock through my window, but then neither would I have let Johnny in the house. Orianna was either quite fearless or she was foolhardy, and it seems to me perfectly in character for her to have shut off all the lights and gone out, unarmed, into the dark. Of course, I have no more idea than you do as to *why* she went out."

"You don't think it was so strange, then?" Sergeant Putnam asked his wife wistfully.

"Not so very," Barbara told him gently.

"You think I'm being obsessive about those lights?"

"Let's say a weeny bit obsessive."

"Mmmmm. But what about Johnny's impression that someone was with her?"

"Impression is the word."

"And if he's right?"

"Dave, Johnny Sparhawk was on his way home from a tavern. It's my bet he spent half the afternoon drinking to get up the nerve to go see Orianna, and God knows how much more he had at Barney's. How do you know he really made that call? How do you know he didn't dream the whole thing? I wouldn't put stock in an *eyewitness* account of Johnny's, much less an impression."

"Okay," Sergeant Putnam said sheepishly. "We'll forget the visitor."

"And the lights?"

"And the lights," he agreed, though somewhat less firmly.

"He was right about one thing," Barbara told him. "Orianna *could* have written a blockbuster of a book on the basis of nothing but Sparhawks. I've found an absolute goldmine in Asa Sewall's, *Memoirs of a Reluctant Rustic.* For instance, he describes his hesitancy, as a child, to pass the Coffin homestead because of their simple-minded son, a young man who, as he puts it, made 'gibberish noises and monkey faces.'"

"You know, I remember Bea once mentioning a retarded Coffin, but that one was a woman—Gil's great-aunt, it must have been. She was hidden away during the daytime but was sometimes seen walking in the yard in the moonlight."

"Poor thing."

"And of course there's Terry."

"Interesting, isn't it? Do you suppose that's why Gil reacted so strongly to Orianna's book? The Bowers have a scandal, too, believe it or not. Their grandfather's first wife was found dead in Alder Brook one

November day in 1895. She was carrying a little basket of goodies and wearing a bright blue cloak. Apparently, she slipped on the frozen surface of the log bridge. Only twenty-four years old and, according to Asa, as pretty as a sunrise."

"So where's the scandal?"

"There was only one house across the brook at the end of that path, Dave, and in that house lived a certain William Mottey—young, handsome, unmarried, and of questionable morals."

"Good heavens."

"Grandfather Bower was twenty years older than his wife and sounds as much fun to live with as a sack of turnips. Asa fills a whole page with a list of his virtues, which tended toward the pious, repressive end of the spectrum. He was very big on hard work and sobriety, and there was Lucy Mae as pretty as a sunrise. Grandpa ran a little store out of his house, which Grandma tended, and whenever he went off on one of his buying trips, she skipped across the brook. Asa seems to have no doubts at all about her destination, but being a Victorian, he resorts to euphemisms and innuendos once she's past the threshold. He could only speculate as to what Grandpa felt, but the old man doesn't seem to have been permanently scarred. He remarried soon afterward, raised a family, and lived to a ripe old age."

"You're really getting into this, aren't you?" Sergeant Putnam asked with some amusement.

"Do you mind?"

"Not if you keep feeding me the juicy bits."

CHAPTER 15

Sᴇʀɢᴇᴀɴᴛ ᴘᴜᴛɴᴀᴍ ᴀʀʀɪᴠᴇᴅ ʟᴀᴛᴇ at Chapel Road on Thursday morning, having first delivered at the high school his annual address to an upperclass assembly on the consequences of driving drunk. Carefully avoiding pontification, he preferred to rely on a very graphic film, the measure of whose impact was the silence in the auditorium as the images flickered on the screen. As usual, he'd found his exit delayed by the principal, Carl Glass, who took the better part of ten minutes to express his satisfaction with the presentation, it being one of the few during the school year that was not accompanied by a litany of wisecracks.

The bell had rung by the time Sergeant Putnam

pushed open the heavy auditorium doors and started down the long shabby corridor toward the front of the building. Whether by design or accident, Scott Coffin had materialized from an empty classroom and fallen into step beside him. After a few token remarks about the program, Scott turned the conversation to Orianna's literary intentions and made a clumsy attempt to ascertain what, if anything, the police had found in her house in the way of written work, and what they were planning to do with it.

"After all," he'd said earnestly when Sergeant Putnam played dumb, "miracles don't happen twice."

So the town knew, thought Sergeant Putnam as he proceeded toward Chapel Road, that Graham Krumbaecker intended to render publishable anything he could lay his hands on. He wished he could set to rest the minds of his friends and neighbors. Len had said the department could not *deliberately* burn the manuscript—that would be too flagrant—but he was not discounting the possibility that certain pieces of paper might, while sheltered in his own home, meet with an unfortunate accident that would prohibit their inclusion with the rest of Orianna's goods and pieces.

Sergeant Putnam took Orianna's keys from his pocket and unlocked the porch door. The plants had been removed and a light coating of dust had built up on the shiny surfaces. He passed quickly from room to room, finding all in order, relocked the back door, and began with the assurance of uneventful repetition a similar circuit of the outside of the house. Thus, he was startled to come upon a window, one of the den windows at the northeast corner of the house, that showed signs of attempted forced entry. Someone had pried up the metal storm sash and savagely attacked the window frame, gouging out large chips of wood. The dwelling had no alarm system, but drop locks on the inside of the upper frame had frustrated the would-be intruder.

The discovery filled Sergeant Putnam with dismay, raising, as it did, the task of surveillance to a new level of seriousness. Their visitor had not been willing to smash glass to gain entry, but who was to say his determination might not intensify? There was no way the Hampford Police Department could allow Orianna's house to be entered, robbed, or vandalized after it had received specific instructions to prevent just such an occurance. Len was going to hit the ceiling!

He completed his inspection, conscientiously examining every remaining ground-floor window without finding any further signs of attempted penetration, and drove back to the station as the bearer of bad tidings.

Chief Henderson, interrupted in the middle of a clandestine snack of coffee and one of Sonia's doughnuts, hastily swept crumbs of frosting to the floor.

"It's kind of like Russian roulette," Sergeant Putnam said, taking a seat. "Any one of those lumps of dough could prove explosive."

"Mind your own business."

"Lard and chocolate, yum, yum. Wonderful post-operative fare."

"You just wish your system could handle it. How did the assembly go?"

Sergeant Putnam told him. He also told him about his discovery on Chapel Road.

"Shit," said Chief Henderson. "Who do you think it was? Krumbaecker? Mr. X? Merlin on the warpath?

Some greedy juvenile delinquent? How about Verlyn? She knows where the good silver's kept."

"How about anyone in town who's still worrying about Orianna's disclosures?"

"That narrows the field a lot. You know what this means, don't you? We're going to have to watch that place. It's no longer a case of putting on the outside lights and swinging up the driveway on the way home to bed. Somebody's got to pull guard duty, and that somebody looks like you."

Sergeant Putnam respected the inevitability of the choice. He was relatively young, reasonably alert, and, comparatively speaking, a paragon of self-discipline. Everett was not considered for any task that might lead him into temptation, and Ted, although conscientious to a fault while conscious, was prone to doze off during breaks in the action.

"Now, listen, Dave," Chief Henderson said, blessing his sergeant's early departure. "Don't play hero. You get in over your head, you back off and call for help. I'll sleep with my good ear toward the phone."

"I'd rather fight off a blood-crazed psychopath than wake Catherine."

"The hell with Catherine. Think of us. We need a disaster like we need a hole in the head. Just tidy up the matter quickly and cleanly and preferably in one night. Otherwise, you'll be spending a lot of time under the stars."

By ten o'clock that evening, Sergeant Putnam was in complete agreement with Chief Henderson's wishes. How a balmy day could turn so goddamn cold when the sun went down was one of the mysteries of nature. He was wearing a red union suit under his uniform, part of

124

his outfit for Old Timer's hockey, woolen gloves, woolen socks, and a woolen jacket, and still his toes ached and his ears burned. Barbara was right, he should have donned his hunting cap, but somehow he had balked at the prospect of an officer of the law making an arrest in orange earflaps.

His car parked in the Russells' yard, he parked himself on a garden bench nestled in the shrubbery at the side of the garage, from which vantage point he could survey the driveway, the rear of the house, and the back lawn. With flashlight on his lap and hands encasing his tingling ears, he huddled amongst sprays of golden forsythia and the spiky needles of upright yews. The situation was not without its humorous aspects, although amusement, he soon discovered, had a low freezing point. Barbara had thoughtfully provided him with a thermos of hot coffee, and had expressed her sympathy and concern, with no intention, however, of forfeiting her own sleep, and as the minutes ticked by he pictured her with growing envy and resentment crawling into their high four-poster beneath the electric blanket that his Yankee soul had initially scorned as effete and to which he was now addicted.

At eleven o'clock, feeling that his blood was jelling in his veins, a medically imprecise condition to be sure, but one that carried visions of expiration, he slipped from his leafy hideout and, stationing himself behind the garage, put his limbs through a series of silent, slow-motion maneuvers to reassure himself they were still attached to his body. A full moon, a pale spring sphere, was sailing up the eastern sky. Earlier obscured by a thin layer of high clouds, its light now poured forth unobstructed, clarifying the shapes of bushes, trees, and buildings and driving a wary Sergeant Putnam back to his nest.

He took off his gloves to pour himself a cup of coffee and gratefully closed his hands around the warmth of the mug. Sitting and sipping, his mood improved, and he was beginning to feel almost cozy and rather sleepy and not very much concerned with Orianna's house or Orianna's manuscript, when a moving bush jolted him out of his lassitude. The bush had not taken many steps before he perceived, instead of foliage, a human form, male by the size of it, making no special attempts at concealment. The dark shape merged momentarily with the larger bulk of the cherry tree and then reappeared, lumbering like a miniature Bigfoot straight to the den window. A thin beam of light played over the frame, winking off and on as the intruder's position shifted. Sergeant Putnam noiselessly set down his coffee cup and slowly eased himself to a standing position, debating his course of action. Should he burst dramatically from his cocoon of foliage or make an effort to creep closer before disclosing himself? Prudence won out: the tendrils of forsythia that entwined his limbs like octupus tentacles threatened to play havoc with a swift emergence. Quietly, he disentangled himself, and with flashlight in one hand and the other on the butt of his revolver, he padded across the lawn toward his quarry.

Perhaps the trespasser caught a blur of movement from the corner of his eye. Perhaps he simply sensed a presence. Whatever the reason, he extinguished his light and bolted clumsily toward the shelter of a clump of rhododendrons. Simultaneously, Sergeant Putnam flicked on his Eveready and caught the fleeing form in its powerful beam.

Even from the back there was no mistaking the identity of the intruder, and Sergeant Putnam was thrust into a terrible and delicate dilemma. One did not casually arrest the chairman of the board of selectmen for criminal trespass. One did not lightly demand that he halt and explain. Horrible scenarios flashed through Sergeant Putnam's mind: Myron making a fool of him in court, insisting—and how could anyone refute his claim?—that he had merely been carrying out a personal inspection in the face of police negligence. Oh, the embarrassment of a confrontation; the possible jeopardy to a job that suddenly looked terribly desirable and upon which the material well-being of his family depended.

Len would not want Myron arrested. This conviction became a resolution in the few seconds it took his prey to crash into and out of several flowering shrubs as he began a hasty retreat across the open lawn. No, he would not, *could* not, confront Myron Streeter. But, by God, he would give him something to remember. And with his decision made, Sergeant Putnam sprinted gleefully after Myron's receding form, goading him onward with periodic stabs of illumination.

Myron galloped to the end of the lawn and plunged into the woods. He was about thirty feet ahead of Sergeant Putnam and twenty or thirty feet to his left. The woods effectively swallowed him from sight, but the crashing, cracking, and snapping that issued from its depths gave evidence of a state of total panic. His pursuer had dissolved into laughter at the mental image of Myron thrashing through the bush, and while thus merrily engrossed in the chase, his flashlight seeking the less brambly gaps for his own passage, he

127

caught his foot and went down like a felled oak, nose-diving into the pine needles. The flashlight described a graceful arc and landed with a thud, illuminating a little circle of false lily-of-the-valley.

Whew! Sergeant Putnam caught his breath and crawled to his hands and knees expecting pain at any moment, but he seemed to have escaped without damage, except perhaps to the knees of his trousers. Attempting to pull his right leg forward preparatory to rising, however, he experienced a moment of irrational, spine-tingling horror. *Somebody was holding his ankle.* Swinging around, he focused the beam of light none too steadily on his captive foot and immediately all specters vanished. His ankle's custodian was not a hand, either attached or severed, but a cleverly positioned rabbit snare.

Dammit all, these things were illegal. He tore at it angrily, pulling up the stakes. The rope was tough nylon cord, a couple of strands discolored with dried blood, and he yanked it off his foot in disgust. Myron's thrashing and churning had abated. Beyond the belt of trees a car engine coughed into life. In one of Hampford's dozens of leafy lanes, Myron had hidden his transport. The roar of acceleration carried clearly through the cold night air and diminished rapidly into silence. Sergeant Putnam pictured a weary Myron, a humbled and disheveled Myron, fleeing the scene of his ignominy, and his sinful heart rejoiced. Grinning, the snare dangling from his hand, he retraced his steps toward Orianna's once more tranquil yard.

CHAPTER 16

T HE ALARM CLOCK BROUGHT a very short night to
an end and Sergeant Putnam left for the station feeling
somewhat light-headed. He might legitimately have
spent the morning in bed in compensation for his
nocturnal duty; Chief Henderson would have been the
first to assert his right to do so and aghast if he actually
had. Since Len arose with the roosters, he felt he was
granting Sergeant Putnam a magnificent concession
when he deferred the first phone call of the morning
until eight o'clock.

Sergeant Putnam took his revenge by cruelly prolonging the preliminaries to the identification of his
nighttime visitor. When he finally reached the point of

disclosure, Chief Henderson shot bolt upright and choked on a swallow of coffee.

"Myron Streeter!" he gasped. "And you chased him across the lawn? Our august and pompous chairman haring for cover like a common criminal? He must have been making plans to go over there even while we were meeting. We didn't break up until ten o'clock. In fact, we'd still be there if Bea hadn't grabbed a pen and outlined the most amazing fairy tale, not one sentence of which was historically accurate. Everyone loved it. The pageant is going to be a great success."

"I'm glad to hear it, Len."

"So what do you think? Is Myron going to give it another try?"

"Maybe something a little more subtle when his heartbeat stabilizes. I think it's safe to assume that he won't attempt any more direct assaults. If you want me to stay there tonight, Len, in the hope of catching other fish, I'm going to camp inside. I damn near froze to death last night."

"We've got better things to do with your time. Let's see if Beany will sleep there. We'll call him a night watchman for the record. I'll have to ask Myron if we can take the money out of the emergency fund. Shall I call him or shall I go over to Mount Pleasant and ask him in person?"

"You bastard," said Sergeant Putnam affectionately.

Chief Henderson seemed pleased with the assessment. "I'll tell him we had an attempted break-in. I'll look him right in the eye and watch him turn slightly green and I'll wager anything that he'll stay off our backs for a nice long time. Now, what the hell's that?" he demanded, as Sergeant Putnam opened a brown paper sack and drew out the snare.

"What does it look like? I fell flat on my kisser last night in Orianna's woods when my foot got tangled up in this thing. I'm willing to bet it's not the only one up there, either."

"Dammit, I'm sick and tired of finding illegal traps," Chief Henderson said, his expression matching his words. "The law is the law, by God, and the law says water traps only. A snare, for godsake, the sly bugger. When we get this guy, Dave, we'll throw the book at him. Give me that thing. I'll send it over to the State Police lab and get an official corroboration on these blood stains. You find its owner."

"Just like that."

"You're damn right. And fast, Dave, fast. If this guy goes up in the woods today and finds his snare gone, he's going to wonder, isn't he?"

"I'll bet it isn't the first one he's lost."

"I'm betting on nothing. Besides, you know as well as I do, we only have to *breathe* our interest in something in this town and invisible warning signals speed right to the perpetrator. It's one of the mysteries of small-town life. By tomorrow there won't be a snare in the county. So get out there and hustle. I want this smart-ass lawbreaker."

Impelled by this directive, Sergeant Putnam went straight to Bea Lambert. At one time in his law-enforcement career, he might have crept around in the woods setting elaborate ambushes or wasted an equal amount of effort confronting former transgressors, but he had long since outgrown the need to pamper his ego. It was easier by far, in light of Bea's superior intelligence network, to put the matter into her hands at once, thus saving himself both hours and energy.

Bea was in her backyard planting onion sets, and was somewhat flustered at being discovered bare-legged in muddy boots. Sergeant Putnam gallantly seized the trowel and, kneeling on an old doormat, methodically interred the remainder of the hard little marbles with their papery skin. The soil was as dark and moist and crumbly as a good German chocolate cake.

"You're the answer to a maiden's prayer," Bea told him happily, "although I'm sure you didn't come up here to get me off my knees."

Sergeant Putnam admitted that, pleasant as he found the task, he did have another purpose in mind. He described his discovery in Orianna's woods, without mentioning either his vigil or his quarry.

"What will happen to this person if he's caught?" Bea asked, studying the swollen buds of her grapevine.

Sergeant Putnam knew that her question touched the central and sticky issue. His fellow townsmen regarded the creatures of the fields as the bounty of a beneficent God who had endowed mankind with the hallowed right to supplement its income and supermarket diet with strings of traps set wherever it wanted to set them—on land, in water, or hanging from trees.

The Hampford Police Department, being sworn to uphold the laws of the Commonwealth, found itself in a delicate position, not so much Chief Henderson, who was fighting the immemorial battle of good versus evil and never allowed himself to be diverted by irrelevant issues such as personal hostility or popularity, but definitely Everett, who never rose above personal considerations, and likewise Sergeant Putnam, who was painfully afflicted with the ability to perceive two sides to every issue. Ted was insulated against the wrath and contempt of his neighbors by his empathy with the creatures in the traps. Ted would, and did, without qualms, blast any bunny that came within fifty feet of his prize roses, but that was clean open warfare. Such rabbits had thrown down the gauntlet, as it were. To creep up on them in their placid bunny neighborhoods and there to wreak destruction upon noncombatants, however, was the moral equivalant to Ted of whooshing napalm over little children.

Recognizing Bea's dilemma, Sergeant Putnam was careful to make the most upbeat assessment of the likely outcome of her testimony, short of actual falsehood.

"We'll take him to court just to scare him. He'll probably get probation and pay a fine."

"He won't go to jail?"

"Oh, no."

"Well, a name springs to mind," said Bea with a sigh, "but it shall not pass my lips until I have done further research."

This impressive if somewhat misleading term referred to the process of dredging up the right cronies and coaxing obscure facts from their memories. Sergeant Putnam knew better than to attempt to rearrange the natural order of things: onions first, then research. Bea would contact him in her own good time.

He went home with a clear conscience to await the call, knowing his presence at the station would only make Len fretful. It was far better for his chief's state of mind that he picture Sergeant Putnam furiously detecting, as long as the end results were the same. Pulling into his driveway yawning and blinking and fully intending to grab a quick nap, he perversely snapped into wakefulness as soon as he crossed the threshold. Changing into a sweatshirt and grease-stained, paint-spattered work pants, he placed the kitchen telephone on the windowsill, took a spade into the backyard, and attacked his own neglected garden.

Barbara joined him, rake in hand, on her return from school, while Jenny sat on the back steps and fed milk and cookies to her doll. Sergeant Putnam's late-night adventures, suppressed during the morning's rush, were resurrected for an appreciative audience.

"The funny thing is, Dave, I know what's bothering him. Myron's great-grandfather *did* hide in a pigpen during the Civil War, and so did the old man's two brothers. When they weren't making a dash for the sty they were making big bucks supplying the Union Army. People used to grunt at them for years afterward whenever they met in the street. It all died down in time, of course, as everything does, but the fact that Myron's money was made by a pack of draft dodgers is definitely not compatible with Myron's image."

Bea called at three-thirty, catching Sergeant Putnam, pleasantly sunburned, nodding off in a deck chair. Bea had never quite made peace with the electronic age and approached its instruments warily, as though each possessed a perverse will of its own. Preliminaries were thus protracted in any call from Bea. Once having established his identity to her satisfaction, however, she proceeded straight to the heart of the matter.

"I think it must be Albert Bower. Those few of us who have dined at the Bowers' over the years all have vivid memories of Vesta's rabbit pie. The crust is like asphalt."

Aware of his disappointment, Sergeant Putnam

asked, "What makes you think she doesn't buy the rabbit?"

"As a boy," Bea said firmly, "Albert Bower always had a dead something dangling from his hand or stuffed under his jacket. Certain sly remarks lead me to believe that Albert has not changed his habits. Moreover, he lives directly against that belt of woods."

Yes, there was proximity, as well as the apparent frequency with which the Bowers enjoyed rabbit pie. As it turned out, Len, too, had caught a whiff of the suspicion that had over the years attached itself to Albert's extracurricular activities, and was predisposed to take Sergeant Putnam's conjecture as confirmation of a known fact.

"Always was a sneaky little bugger," was his unprofessional opinion. "We'll need a search warrant. Damn and blast," he said, checking his watch. "Judge Fogg will be off like a rocket at four o'clock, and as for Sawyer, I'll bet he's been on the golf course for an hour. Myron's game is going to be a little shaky tomorrow," he added snidely.

"Your visit upset him, did it?"

"Had him squirming," Chief Henderson recalled with pleasure. "He okayed Beany's recompense without a murmur, promised new rain gear within a week, agreed that we ought to be compensated for the time spent at target practice, and vowed to fight tooth and nail for a new cruiser."

"Some might call that blackmail."

"I prefer to think of it as the triumph of justice," Chief Henderson said modestly. "Anyway, it was probably the happiest half hour of my life."

CHAPTER 17

WHILE CHIEF HENDERSON SEARCHED out judicial authority, Sergeant Putnam and Everett sustained the cause of law and order, each in his own way, Sergeant Putnam tackling overdue paperwork and Everett draping himself across the counter, whence came the surreptitious crackle of candy-bar wrappers. A steel-gray cloud cover had swarmed across the sky's blue dome, and silent silver threads of rain were lacing the windowpanes.

"I hope it's clear on Sunday," Everett said through a mouth full of chocolate.

"What's happening Sunday?"

"Ollie's gettin' christened."

"Which one is Ollie?"

"Melody's."

"Oh."

The Hewitt girls observed one ecclesiastical ritual as scrupulously as they ignored the others. The sacrament of baptism had become an annual orgy of sentimental piety in the Hewitt family, followed by enough ribald revelry to guarantee the repetition of the rites nine months later.

"Oliver Rocco Hewitt."

'That's nice, Ev. Nice ring to it. Good luck to him." Sergeant Putnam told himself to remember the name for Barbara's enjoyment. Her favorites were Tracee's twins, Rexford and Rowena.

Chief Henderson was slow in returning, having tracked Judge Fogg to the barber shop adjacent to the courthouse, where he had waited out a magisterial shave as well as a haircut to procure the warrant. Shortly before five o'clock, Sergeant Putnam and Everett proceeded north on Main Street. They passed Chapel Road on their left, and swung into the Bowers' driveway beneath a venerable sugar maple whose red buds were briefly setting the old tree ablaze.

The house consisted of a poorly proportioned main structure with a compressed upper story and dormers sprouting in all directions. A large kitchen ell and a front porch added to the graceless bulk of the place. Albert planted morning glories along the porch every spring, and his neatly woven web of twine was already strung in preparation for this year's pastel display. A barn, sheathed in white clapboards, stood to the right of the house, and behind it they could glimpse a scattering of outbuildings, all in a state of good repair, a large vegetable garden, a small meadow, and the verge of the woods that stretched between Chapel Road and Route 117 in a long green tunnel all the way to Apple Valley.

"It's no friggin' White House."

"It means a lot to them, Ev," Sergeant Putnam replied mildly. "They've been here four or five generations."

"These old wrecks," Everett grumbled, splashing behind his superior, "they oughta be leveled."

Already familiar with Everett's views on aging, Sergeant Putnam declined to ascertain whether this remark referred to the house or its inhabitants. His knock on the kitchen door was followed by a considerable delay before the door swung open and Vesta peered at them uncertainly, wiping her hands on her apron. Her eyes darted to the cruiser and back to the two policemen.

"What's the matter?" she asked in a high, breathless voice. "Have I done something wrong?"

"Not that I know of, Miss Bower. May we come in for a minute?"

"Why, I guess you may. Yes, come out of the rain. I'll go call Harley. Excuse the mess, I was doing some baking."

The term appeared to be a synonym for chaos. Flour had drifted from the top of the wooden cooking table across the worn linoleum floor, the old granite sink was piled with a hodgepodge of utensils, bowls, and baking sheets, an unappetizing-looking grayish batter had dripped down the front of one of the cupboards, and smoke was seeping from the oven of a mammoth wood and gas range.

"Excuse me, Miss Bower," Everett said after several explosive coughs, "but whatever's in that oven is cryin' to come out."

"Oh, no, I don't think so," Vesta Bower said, dithering between the stove and the doorway to the hall. "I know when a cake is done. Harley is changing. He'll be right down."

"It's Albert we've come to see. Is he at home?" Sergeant Putnam asked.

"He's out in his workshop," Vesta replied, patently surprised by his request. "Down back of the barn."

"Ev, go keep him company." If Albert was truly positioned behind the barn, the odds were good that he had failed to observe the cruiser's arrival. Still, Sergeant Putnam was assuming nothing. Everett, with streaming eyes, fled gratefully into the rain.

"What do you want with Albert?" demanded Harley Bower, fastening the last button of his cardigan as he entered the kitchen.

"Your brother Albert is suspected of doing some poaching in the woods out back. It appears he's been setting rabbit snares, which, as I'm sure you know, is illegal."

"Rabbit snares!" Harley repeated with a snort of amusement. At least, he *seemed* to be smiling; it was difficult to discern his expression through the haze. "You expect he'll tell you if he has?"

"No, I don't. That's why I have a search warrant."

The Bowers stiffened at that bit of news. Nobody likes a search warrant; God knows what pathetic habits or possessions might be scrutinized by cold eyes.

"I'd like to see that warrant," Harley said firmly

after a moment, and Vesta shot him a glance of respect. He was as good as a lawyer, Harley was, for knowing the rights of the common man and not letting the authorities roll right over him.

Sergeant Putnam produced the document and Harley inspected it, according Judge Fogg's signature a respectful nod.

"It's in order," he said regretfully. "I suppose you want to look around Albert's workshop. I'll show you the way."

While Harley unhooked an umbrella from a peg by the door, Vesta scurried to the stove and yanked from the oven a pan of some blackened mess, which she then dumped unceremoniously on the drainboard to cool. Neither she nor Harley expressed the slightest concern about the well-done condition of the contents of the pan, but Sergeant Putnam, who followed the siblings into the yard, marveled that any of the Bowers had survived past youth.

Harley had chosen a decorous black umbrella. Vesta's little cover, with its blood-red spots, resembled a gaudy, poisonous toadstool. The three of them trotted single file down a path along the edge of a lawn whose central feature was a mammoth clothesline strung on posts that appeared embedded for eternity. Directly behind the barn, across from a hen yard, was a sturdy weathered shed that might have once been a machine shed but was now Albert's workshop. Harley, in the lead, closed his umbrella, pressed down on the thumb latch of the door, and stood back to allow the rest of the party passage within.

Everett, looking painfully bored, had planted his rump on the edge of the workbench in front of which

Albert was perched on a stool, working diligently with an awl on a strip of leather. The youngest Bower, dressed in a gray sweatshirt and overalls, glanced up from his task to survey them briefly with mild blue eyes. Aside from the workbench and a kerosene heater, also illegal, the room was a jumble of scrap lumber, boxes, broken furniture, and discarded tools. Shelves held rusted cans of "parts," dusty balls of string, and jars of nails and screws in every conceivable size. An ancient suit of canvas rain gear hung on a wall alongside a moldy life jacket. There were snowshoes without their webbing, baskets full of rat holes, and a hand-carved oxen yoke. Albert was a saver.

"Albert, you don't have to say a word," Harley told him quickly.

"Don't intend to," Albert replied, intent on his handiwork.

"Mr. Bower, I'll have to ask you to stay out of this," said Sergeant Putnam firmly. "As a rabbit pie eater, you are an accessory after the fact. Albert, are you setting snares in the woods?"

"What?"

"Snares. For rabbits. We found one."

"Prove it's mine."

"That's exactly what I'm going to do," Sergeant Putnam snapped. "Ev, start in that corner and I'll take this one."

"He has a search warrant," Harley explained, retrieving a sickle from Albert's workbench and returning it to its peg.

"Mr. Bower, please keep yours hands at your sides," Sergeant Putnam said.

"Well, I never," gasped Vesta. "If your mother could hear you now, David Putnam."

"Give a man a taste of power," Harley intoned," and he'll soon be stepping on the backs of his friends."

Sergeant Putnam heard this pronouncement with particular annoyance. He had just banged his head on an overhanging bicycle wheel and walked into a cobweb. Dust flew up from every disarranged surface. Everett was racked by several horrendous sneezes.

In the end it was Harley who led them to the rope. He seemed to be playing Red Light. Every time Sergeant Putnam turned his back he sensed a shuffling movement on Harley's part, but his quickest glance caught Harley standing as meekly as Vesta, except that he was a little closer to the far end of the workbench. His curiosity aroused, Sergeant Putnam strode over to scan the area of interest and discovered, looped over a nail driven into the end of the bench, a coil of rope that looked awfully similar to the rope from which the snare had been fashioned. He had removed the coil from the nail and was running it through his hands in front of the studiously disinterested Bowers when Everett, still rooting in the far corner, jumped six inches.

"Jesus H. Christ," he bellowed.

"What's the matter?"

"It snapped at me," Everett cried, pointing toward the corner while attempting to scale the workbench in hasty retreat.

Sergeant Putnam pushed past him impatiently, following the line of his outstretched finger. Being familiar with Everett's timidity in the face of wildlife of any kind, he fully expected to find a combative field mouse. Instead, he distinguished, behind a pile of musty burlap bags, a gleaming white object, which, upon closer inspection, he defined as an animal skull. Curious, he picked it up and carried it toward stronger light.

143

"Lucky it didn't take off your hand," he told Everett solemnly.

"It did too snap," Everett replied sullenly.

The thing had a broad head and a long jaw and a set of teeth like a hay rake. "What is it?" Sergeant Putnam asked, turning the skull in his hands.

"It's great-grandpa's wolf head," Vesta explained with obvious pride. "I don't know what it's doing out here, though."

"Now wait a minute. This thing belonged to your great-grandfather?"

"He killed the wolf."

Sergeant Putnam made some quick calculations. Assuming a birthdate between 1820 and 1830, great-grandpa's wolf-bagging days would have fallen somewhere around mid-century. Were there wolves in Massachusetts in 1850? he asked himself. He thought not. What else could it be? A big dog? A badger? It certainly looked like a wolf, or what he imagined a wolf should look like. Had great-grandpa capitalized on an ancestor's prowess, taking credit where credit wasn't due?

That the Bowers shared none of his doubts was apparent in the fond looks they cast on the object, although Harley and Vesta appeared somewhat perturbed at finding the skull in the shed. Albert, however, had a ready explanation.

"I was cleaning it," he said, and they nodded understandingly. It was apparently the kind of task a Bower legitimately, and even commendably, undertook.

Sergeant Putnam, in the deliberately obtuse manner of a policeman, demanded clarification of the obvious. "It's not usually here in the workshop, then?"

"Oh, no," Vesta answered, shocked that he would

144

think they'd be so careless with a meaningful heirloom. "Goodness, no, it has its own shelf in the attic."

Well, that was okay, Sergeant Putnam told himself. He'd half expected to hear that it hung on the dining room wall, baring its savage grin while the living ate, or reposed on a coffee table with ivy twining between its impressive choppers. He laid it down on the workbench with the care befitting a precious relic and retrieved the rope that was, after all, the item he'd come to collect. The coil, he quickly discovered, did not consist of one long piece but of at least half a dozen shorter lengths. Examining these segments, he was delighted to find on one a long reddish-brown stain. Albert, it seemed, was crafty enough to disassemble his snares for storage but apparently considered it safe to recycle the rope.

"Well, this should do it," he said cheerfully, earning a reproachful glance from Vesta and an angry stiffening of Albert's back. Harley adopted a more ambiguous attitude. Being employed in the halls of justice, he could not appear to condone his brother's disregard of municipal ordinances. Yet Sergeant Putnam found it hard to believe that Harley had eaten rabbit pie and rabbit stew month after month, year after year, in total ignorance of its origin. No wonder he looked a little discomforted.

"Well, well," Harley said vaguely, trailing Sergeant Putnam and Everett out of the workshop, and this enigmatic utterance proved to be his sole comment on the situation. He and Vesta escorted the two policemen back to the crusier in leaden silence and oversaw their departure while Harley's umbrella dripped steadily onto his sister's, a foot below.

Chief Henderson was so delighted with the rope that he found it difficult to let go of it, and dispatched Everett to the lab with a string of admonitions ringing in his ears.

"I suppose we won't hear anything until next week, but time doesn't matter now. We've got him. Don't you think so, Dave? Didn't those ropes look identical to you?"

"There's no doubt in my mind, Len. And there was none in Harley's either."

"I've known Harley Bower all my life," mused Chief Henderson, "and yet I really don't know him at all. I was in Vesta's class at school. She was a serious little thing. Then there was Margaret, the one who died young. I always liked Margaret. Harley was a helluva marble player, a gawky kid, all legs and nose."

"How about Albert?"

"Little baby Albert carried a slingshot in his back pocket and damn near put my eye out one day. My old man marched over there and let his old man have a few choice words, and Albert went right on plugging everything that moved. Well, now I'm getting my own back," Chief Henderson said with a laugh. "It's only taken me sixty years."

CHAPTER 18

SERGEANT PUTNAM AWOKE ON Saturday filled with the pleasurable anticipation of a weekend without work. Matching his mood, the sun was shining, the sky arched cloudless, and a moderate breeze kept the black flies down. He and Barbara spent a busy morning without once crossing paths, a not unusual Saturday occurrence. It was noontime before they said good morning.

"Daddy," Jenny cried, popping out of the car upon her return from gymnastics class. "We're going to be in the play, me and Mummy. We're going to be old-fashioned people and I have to wear a costume."

"No kidding? And Mummy, too?"

"Mummy too," Barbara confirmed. "Bea called this morning. We have our first rehearsal this afternoon." The boys went their own ways on Saturdays, and Jenny raced next door to deliver the news to her best friend. Sergeant Putnam made a couple of mammoth sandwiches, and he and Barbara took their lunch outside to the picnic table, loathe to waste a moment of the sunshine.

"Any more sordid bits of town lore?" he asked her, nipping into his liverwurst.

Barbara looked slightly abashed. "I think my research is over, Dave. I was beginning to pursue it a little too avidly. You know, some things are better left alone. There *is* a strange matter I came across last night and can't get out of my mind, though. Before I put everything away, I read through Orianna's notes again—I hadn't done that before, not carefully. I read the manuscript, but I just skimmed the notes. Anyway, I found a mention of Lucy Mae Bower—I told you her story, remember? Orianna called her Lucinda Maude. If that's her idea of a disguised name, we're awfully lucky she never got to finish her book. In any case, Lucy, or Lucinda, was going to meet what's-his-name—that appears to be documented fact—and was found lying in the brook, which confirms Asa Sewall's account. But in Orianna's version her throat had been slashed and she bled to death. The attack was attributed to a wild beast. Orianna blamed a wolf."

Sergeant Putnam set down the remainder of his sandwich. His voice, when he spoke, sounded hollow even to his own ears. "Then which one is the true story?"

"I don't know. I don't know whether Orianna found

another source or whether it was simply a product of her imagination. But it's been haunting me since last night. Because, of course, of the similarity to her own death."

"Barbara, I've got something I've got to do," he said, rising. "May I take the car?"

"Yes, of course. Jenny and I can walk to the rehearsal. Is something the matter, Dave? You sound funny."

"I'm not surprised," he said. "I might be going crazy."

Leaving her with these words of comfort, he backed the car into Cedar Avenue and drove toward Main Street waging an internal battle between the possibility of his indeed being completely irrational and the possibility of his being incredibly, improbably right.

Asa Sewall's story, he told himself with the wisdom of hindsight, had never appeared completely convincing. "Bridge" was probably a grandiose designation for a couple of logs thrown across the stream. Even if Lucy Mae had come skipping along at a pretty jolly pace, it was hard to imagine how she could have incurred more than a few bruises, or perhaps a broken arm, in a fall from that height, especially padded by her new blue cloak. Alder Brook was at no spot along its rather marshy length lined with any quantity of rocks. What were the chances of her head coming down on one? Of course, in the space of almost a hundred years, all kinds of changes might have taken place, from a diversion of the stream bed to the removal of rocks for wall building. He was letting himself float into conjecture if he based his conclusions on a hundred-year-old land-scape.

What he did know was this: when Barbara had said "wolf," he'd seen a vision of Orianna's throat. Shades of Everett! But on the way home from the Bowers' hadn't Ev referred to the wolf's skull as a death's head, a comment that Sergeant Putnam had countered with a facetious remark, it being impossible for him to receive Everett's confidences without acute embarrassment, partially or even primarily, he suspected, because of the temple in which these perceptions dwelt—the ever-festering acne, the greasy hair, the little roll of fat around the waist.

Resolutely, he discarded the inexplicable and embraced the substantive. If Lucy Mae had not slipped off the bridge and knocked herself unconscious on a rock and drowned in shallow Alder Brook, if something more definitive had taken care of Lucy Mae, then that something was not a wolf. Despite the grisly convictions of its inhabitants, the forests of Massachusetts contained no wolves in 1891, that he had ascertained beyond a doubt. There were, in fact, few forests, far fewer than at present, and in those that remained all fierce beasts had been exterminated with Yankee efficiency. So how about a wolf's skull with gleaming white teeth? Wasn't that the possibility he was gingerly approaching? A wolf's skull had belonged to Grandpa Bower, who was blatantly being deceived, and Lucy Mae had died of a "wolf" attack. These two facts, if true, were inescapably linked.

Not that he expected the skull, after all these years, to count as admissible evidence, but surely he ought to test its capabilities. If those fangs were too blunt to rip a Kleenex, much less a throat, his theory flew out the window, and he'd better ask Len for a leave of absence until his feverish imagination cooled down.

He resorted, in the end, to the saving virtue of thoroughness. A policeman could never go wrong being thorough. So he was merely demonstrating a conscientious and commendable application to duty when he parked once again in the Bowers' driveway and approached the house.

The Bowers were engaged in a communal rite of spring that was being duplicated all over town: they were taking down their storm windows, theirs being the heavy, wooden, old-fashioned kind that had to be installed or removed twice a year. Albert was standing on a ladder, Harley strategically positioned below him, while Vesta, with ammonia and rags, was scouring a rain-streaked pane.

They suspended their activity when Sergeant Putnam appeared and regarded his advance neutrally. Since there existed no credible excuse for the request he was about to make other than the truth, he dispensed with any attempt at explanations and simply asked.

"Sorry to bother you folks again, but I'd like to borrow that wolf's skull of yours for a couple of days."

He was holding his breath, but he needn't have. No one demanded why or asked on whose authority. Instead, to his great surprise, the two men turned back to their tasks as though the matter had lost their interest.

"I thought you wanted it for the length of the pageant," Vesta said. "That's what Bea told me."

"Oh, did she?"

"Anyway, she's already picked it up, David. I guess you got your signals crossed."

"I guess we did, all right, Miss Bower. Thanks anyway."

He refused to gape in front of the Bowers. Whatever Bea's motive in obtaining the skull, she had approached the task a lot more skillfully than he had. It seemed irrelevant at this point whether she had, in all innocence, requested the relic as a dramatic prop, or whether she had duplicated his line of reasoning and was, as usual, skipping two steps ahead of him down the trail.

He was almost at the end of the walk when Albert shouted, "When do I get my rope back, David Putnam?"

"You'll get it back when we're through with it," Sergeant Putnam replied shortly.

"My, that's an important piece of rope."

"Hush, Albert," Vesta scolded, and Sergeant Putnam trundled back to his car fighting an impulse to give Albert a good swift kick in the rear.

Discovering his house unoccupied, he proceeded straight to the town hall on the assumption that the rehearsal had started and Bea could be found at its helm. He found at least a quarter of the population of Hampford milling around on the second floor in a large chamber whose decor, stylish in 1890, consisted of a good deal of shiny, varnished woodwork and three hideous chandeliers. The folding chairs had been stacked against the walls, and Laurel Bradford was standing on the stage with a megaphone calling out names, in response to which the designated moved to the right, left, or back of the room, gradually coalescing into separate groups.

Sergeant Putnam spotted Bea at the foot of the stage

with a sheaf of papers in her hand at the very moment that Jenny hurled herself into his arms. After disentangling himself from her zealous embrace, he sent her skipping back to Barbara, who was chatting with friends and contented herself with a wave.

"Why, David," Bea said with feigned surprise, thereby establishing her guilt. She was wearing her basketball sneakers, and several pencils were skewered in workmanlike fashion through her gray curls.

"I'd appreciate it, Bea," Sergeant Putnam said sternly, "if you would let the police department know when you're working on a case. I've just been out to the Bowers', where I found that a certain active elder citizen had already paid a call."

"I was going to rush right over after rehearsal," Bea assured him. "The idea came to me at four o'clock this morning—I'm usually wrestling with the problems of the world at that hour—and I decided that I'd feel better if I had the thing right under my nose. It's out back with the other props. I promised them it would be prominently displayed. They were flattered."

"I suppose you think you were pretty clever."

"I don't think I did too badly," Bea said modestly. "You take it right along. I only got it for you. When I heard yesterday evening that you and Everett had stumbled over that old skull out in the shed while you were looking for Albert's snares, I perked up like a bird dog on a scent, because the Bowers treat that piece of bone like a member of the family. Bea, I said to myself, it's very strange that their precious skull was kicking around Albert's old workshop and furthermore, why was Albert cleaning it? Because that's the story I heard, that when you asked him why it was out there, he said he was cleaning it, and Vesta and Harley not even knowing he had it. Why in the world *any* of them have held onto it is beyond me. I can't imagine who in his right mind would want a memento of that horrid old man. He abused his wife and children, you know. Father was a witness to that. Dear Father had nothing but contempt for the official version of Lucy Mae's death. 'Hogwash,' he called it.''

"He didn't believe it was an accident?"

"Nor did many others at the time. I happened just this morning to pay a visit to Annie Staples, who having just recently entered her ninety-ninth year is now Hampford's oldest inhabitant and still sharp as a tack, and she agreed with Father's assessment. One day her little white dog got in Grandpa Bower's path and the old man lifted the animal on the toe of his boot and sent it halfway across the street. And *smiled*. I rest my case.''

"You think he really cut her throat?"

Bea regarded him blankly. "It wasn't her throat, David, it was her head. Her head was bashed in with an effectiveness that couldn't have occurred in a fall from anything less than the Empire State Building.''

It was Sergeant Putnam's turn to look puzzled. "Then why did you get the skull?"

"Why, because of Orianna. You have to have proof. You can't just accuse him. Don't you think you should get it to the lab right away?"

Ted, who was on duty, said he thought Chief Henderson had gone to the boat show in Bristol, so Sergeant Putnam borrowed one of Ted's maxims, "In for a penny, in for a pound," and dropped the skull off at the lab himself along with a plea for expeditious handling, after which he retired to his backyard and calmed himself down by putting in three rows of beets and lettuce before Barbara and Jenny returned from the rehearsal.

Barbara appeared somewhat bemused by her experience.

"It's a little like a seventeenth-century *Annie*. Merlin has volunteered to play Chief Running Bird, Myron is clamoring to portray Peletiah Birdlime. Bea's made *everyone* a hero, that's the secret, with each one outdoing the next in nobility and no one bearing the slightest resemblance to any historical figure. Even the casting was a model of efficiency. All us brunettes are Indians; the blonds are settlers."

CHAPTER 19

SUNDAY MORNING PRESENTED AN overcast sky and a steady, trickling rain, as if someone had left a shower dribbling. Relieved of the possibility of outdoor chores, Sergeant Putnam was prolonging his breakfast over a second cup of coffee and the *Boston Globe* when Chief Henderson called. Reluctantly withdrawing his attention from the sports section, he picked up Len in midsentence.

". . . not my rope, oh no, they'd never heard of that. This was an object delivered by my sergeant yesterday afternoon with a demand for top priority. How do you suppose I felt when Walfield called this morning and I didn't know what he was talking about?"

"I never thought it would be done so fast," Sergeant Putnam said as he studied a photograph of a seventeen-year-old high school basketball player who had thirty-four college scholarship offers. The kid wore size-sixteen sneakers. Sergeant Putnam tried to visualize a foot as long as a doll's bed.

"'It's about the skull, Chief,'" Walfield said to me, 'that your sergeant brought in yesterday.' 'Oh, *that* skull,' I answered. Now, what I want to know from *you*," Len roared, "is where the hell that skull came from? Because that skull has human blood on it, Dave. Are you listening to me? Someone recently scrubbed that skull, but not well enough. Some of the blood had dried in the crevices of the tooth sockets. B positive blood, Dave."

"I hear you."

"All this means something to you, does it?"

"It's the Bowers' wolf skull, Len. It belonged to their great-grandfather."

"This blood isn't that old, Dave."

"No, the blood is Orianna's."

"I see," Chief Henderson said quietly. He dropped his bluster very quickly when circumstances demanded a professional approach. "I'll swing by and pick you up."

"I guess it's a good thing you *didn't* tell me yesterday," he said ten minutes later, having listened to Sergeant Putnam's story. "Can you imagine my reaction?" He shook his head as though awed himself by the speculation of such an eruption.

"I might have suspected Everett of being contagious," the chief continued. "Even now, with the proof in front of me, I find the idea preposterous. But dammit, we have Orianna's blood type on the teeth of whatever the hell this animal is, and that's a fact that compels some respect."

The degree of his concern was reflected in his appearance. While Sergeant Putnam wore slacks and a windbreaker, Chief Henderson had donned his full uniform. Garbed in official attire, he became more patriotic, more indomitable, more courageous, as the situation warranted.

Viewing the Bowers' empty barn, he said, "Still at church, I guess. If I hadn't played hookey, I could have confronted them right in the vestry."

Sergeant Putnam checked his watch. He was a Christmas–Easter–Children's Day celebrant himself. "Quarter of eleven. They ought to be home soon, Vesta and Albert, anyway. Harley goes to some tabernacle thing in Mount Pleasant."

"That's right, he does. Someone must get a ride with another party. What time is the service at the temple?"

"Tabernacle."

"Whatever."

"I don't know."

They approached the kitchen door, where Chief Henderson rapped and then jiggled the knob without raising a response.

"Let's take a look around while we're waiting. I'd like to see the shop."

Once again Sergeant Putnam trod the path between house and barn. Against the inside back wall of the latter, the storm windows were neatly stacked, numbered, he was willing to bet, according to some esoteric system handed down from generation unto generation of Bowers. A border of bricks set at an angle contained the back lawn, within which uncompromising barrier, each and every blade of grass conformed to Bower specifications, and outside of which, not one blade strayed. It was an eminently tidy yard, a utilitarian yard. He was struck by its lack of flowers.

"This may be locked up, too," he warned Chief Henderson as they approached the shed, but the door opened easily on well-oiled hinges. He stopped so suddenly on the threshold, checked by the obscurity within, that Chief Henderson ran up his heels. Then, realizing in the instant it took his eyes to adjust to the gloom what it was that was blocking the light from the window, Sergeant Putnam lunged forward, bringing another exclamation from his chief, who came hurtling after him. But they were too late.

"Goddamn," said Chief Henderson softly. "Why did he have to do this?"

Together they cut down the body of Harley Bower, who was wearing his Sunday suit and had been dead for some time. There was no question of resuscitation.

"Goddamn," Chief Henderson repeated. Then he took a clean burlap bag and covered Harley's face.

Sergeant Putnam sat down on Albert's stool. The sight of Harley's thin hands laying flat on the splintered wooden floor disturbed him more than Harley's distorted face. "I thought it was Albert."

"Who says it wasn't," Chief Henderson said. He sounded angry. "Harley is just the kind of dutiful, deluded bugger who would lay down his life for his brother."

"On the other hand . . ."

"That's right, the other hand is entirely possible, too. Family honor, et cetera, et cetera. What a stupid waste."

"I guess we'll have to tell Vesta and Albert."

"Yes, we will, but there's no reason why they have to see him like this. We'll go back to the house and wait. There's plenty of time to get the official machinery rolling. Harley's not going anywhere."

A sudden splattering shower chased them off the kitchen steps, however, and sent them running back to the barn, where they stood in the doorway watching water drip from the eaves until the Bowers' Plymouth rolled into the yard, Vesta all but hidden behind the wheel. Chief Henderson insisted that they all move into the kitchen before he broke the news. Then he seated Vesta in her rocker and told her that Harley was dead. A little sound escaped from Vesta, who sat absolutely still, as though to freeze the pain, while Albert moved to the window and gazed out at the yard to hide his tears.

"I'll have to talk to you later, Vesta," Chief Henderson said gently.

"I understand."

"But there's no rush. You take all the time you need. Dave is going to call Clint Pearson, and Clint and I will arrange for an ambulance."

Gradually it all became real. The two remaining Bowers seemed very small and vulnerable, and sought comfort in proximity, as Dr. Pearson banged in and out, robust and hearty in the face of death. Far from deploring his lack of sensitivity, Hampfordites admired this aspect of his personality, as though his coarse, exuberant energy was evidence of his fitness to tackle the forces of disease and decay. Take that, cancer! A straight left for heart disease; a knockout blow to clogged arteries.

Dr. Pearson held Vesta's hands and told her she was a brave little body and clapped Albert on the back and said he was a good soldier. Car doors slammed in the yard, the ambulance came and went, large men tramped through the kitchen. As quickly as the flurry of activity had begun, it died away, and there was nothing else to do but leave Vesta and Albert to their grief. Chief Henderson suggested that he return after a decent interval to ask his questions in the sanctuary of their home, but Vesta said they weren't in the habit of being indulged and if their duty lay in a trip to the police station, they were ready to go.

Resolutely, they clambered into the back of the cruiser, neither feeling steady enough to drive, and sat shoulder to shoulder, Vesta clutching her white plastic Sunday handbag and Albert in a blue pinstripe whose sleeves were too long. Neither spoke during the journey but regarded the passing landscape with set faces.

CHAPTER 20

NOT AT ALL TO Sergeant Putnam's surprise, they found Bea Lambert in attendance at the station, breaking the monotony of the Sabbath for a visibly grateful Ted. Bea was wearing a church dress of flowered polyester and had spread her raincape on the counter to dry, a familiarity that Chief Henderson greeted with a snarl. His asperity subsided, however, when Bea produced a thermos of hot tea, a cup of which, well-sweetened, brought the color back to Vesta's cheeks and primed her faculty of speech. Albert stared at his large rough hands, one planted firmly on each knee, and retreated from participation. Had they in Albert's case, Sergeant Putnam wondered, mistaken craftiness for intelligence?

"From the time he was a little boy, Harley watched over the rest of us," Vesta told them sorrowfully.

"He was a wonderful brother," Bea affirmed to a round of solemn nods.

"He was so worried when he heard about Mrs. Soule's book. He worried himself sick. Because he took his responsibilities to heart, being the eldest son and all."

"I seem to remember that he had a terrible cold at the time of her death," Bea said sympathetically.

"He was in a state," Vesta agreed, "body and soul."

"And still he went out that cold spring night feeling so sick?" Bea asked slyly.

"Harley never let physical weakness stand in the way of duty," Vesta stated with a touch of pride. "He started to get better right away afterward. It was weighing on his mind so much, what she might say about us in her book, that when she was gone he couldn't help but feel better. He was so happy that afternoon sorting his stamps."

"Yet by this morning," Chief Henderson chipped in, "he was a desperate man. Did he indicate in any way last night that he knew we suspected him? Did he do anything out of the ordinary?"

Vesta thought hard. "He had two helpings of bread pudding," she said at last.

"I don't think he knew last night," Bea said, "and I'll tell you why. Nestor Wimble was a friend of Harley's, wasn't he, Vesta?"

"In a manner of speaking," Vesta said tartly. "He's the one who introduced Harley to the Tabernacle."

"And Harley rode with him on Sundays?"

"He did. Their service is earlier than ours, but not so

164

early that Harley could get back in time for Albert and me to go to ours."

"Nestor Wimble was at the town hall yesterday for the rehearsal," Bea explained. "Besides taking part as one of the settlers, he helped me carry boxes from my car and was in and out of the back room all afternoon. He noticed the skull and, naturally, was curious about it. I'm sure he would have raised the subject with Harley this morning, and if he saw David take away the skull, which I think he must have, that information would also have been passed along."

"Oh, poor Harley," Vesta said, her voice beginning to quaver. "He must have been so frightened."

While Bea offered a comforting hand, Chief Henderson deftly diverted the focus of the questioning. "Here's a question for you, Albert. What I don't understand is why, if your brother used the skull, you cleaned it?"

"He was cleaning it himself one morning, early, out in my shed, and I said I would finish the job because he had to go to work. He was getting water on his good suit."

"How long was this after Mrs. Soule's death?"

"Pretty long after."

"Next day? Next week?"

"I don't remember."

"Did he tell you why he was cleaning it?"

"Said it was dirty."

"But when Sergeant Putnam found the skull in your workshop, Harley seemed surprised."

"Prob'ly was. I forgot to put it back."

"Did your brother seem worried and depressed to you, Albert, before Mrs. Soule died?"

"Oh, yes, worried and depressed."

"What was it he was so afraid Mrs. Soule was going to write about?"

The two Bowers withdrew almost visibly into silence.

Bea, who was refilling Vesta's mug, said casually, "Don't tell me it was that old business about Lucy Mae."

Her statement pierced their defenses like an arrow. Albert's head jerked up. Vesta blanched. "Who knows about that?" she cried in alarm.

"Very few people," Chief Henderson assured her soothingly. "And anyway, Vesta, it seems to me that the case against your grandfather was never proven one way or the other."

"Oh, we knew the truth," Vesta said bitterly. "Papa saw to that. He had a terrible fear that Grandpa's tendency would show itself in one of us. That's why he made us promise not to marry, so as not to carry on the taint. And you see," she added sadly, "he was right. Harley did have the tendency."

Bea and Ted took the Bowers home, and Bea made a phone call on her return to the president of the Friendly Wheel that ensured they would be deluged with baked goods, sympathy, and more company than they had entertained in forty years.

"She's afraid," Bea said after she hung up, handing a mug of tea to Ted, who was brooding about the death of an innocent dog. "She's afraid that the Tabernacle will claim him, but she's determined to give him a Congregational burial. "

"She seems to have no doubts that Harley is the one with the 'tendency,' as she so delicately put it," Chief Henderson said.

166

"And do you have doubts?" Bea asked shrewdly.

"Let's say I have questions. C'mon, Ted, mistakes happen. It could have been a human being."

If this was intended to comfort Ted, it completely backfired, since Ted assigned human beings a rather low rung on the ladder of moral worth. Bea and Sergeant Putnam sent emphatic signals to Chief Henderson that his intervention was only making things worse, a conclusion he accepted with obvious exasperation.

"I'm not satisfied about that skull," he said. "Where was it between the night Harley supposedly used it and the morning Albert claims he was cleaning it?"

"Couldn't Harley have hidden it somewhere on the night of her death, Len? Remember, he was feeling pretty sick. Then, later, he realized it couldn't just disappear like that, that sooner or later his brother and sister were going to miss it. So he dragged it out and Albert found him cleaning it."

"Or he came upon Albert cleaning it."

"But Albert would have had all day to do it. Why would he haul it out in front of Harley?"

"He panicked and went to big brother for help."

"Or thought that Harley would approve."

"I wonder who threw the stone," said Bea, "Harley or Albert?"

"Who says it was either one?"

"What I wonder is how he got Orianna to come out of the house."

"I've been thinking about that," Ted offered gravely, stimulated, for the moment at least, out of his mourning. "I've been thinking how I would have done it, if I had done it, which, of course, I didn't. First thing, I'd have made friends with Prince, maybe taking along a little piece of juicy steak or some lean hamburger and feeding him when he came out before bedtime. Of course, I would have realized right away," he added with a significant glance at Chief Henderson, "that here was a dog who would never hurt a fly. But I wouldn't know that the first night, so I'd have been sure to furnish a little treat."

"Then, on the following night, the dog would have known me and come right to me. There would have been no problem putting a rope on him and tying him up in the woods. That's where he got the rope fibers in his teeth, by the way, getting bored and chewing on the rope while he waited for Harley to come back. Well, with the dog out of the way, I would have gone to the door and knocked or rung the bell. I think she has a bell, doesn't she, Dave?"

Sergeant Putnam affirmed the presence of a bell. Ted's recitals were notoriously scrupulous and exasperatingly accurate.

"When she came to the door, I would have introduced myself. 'I'm Ted Deegan, ma'am.' Of course Harley wouldn't have said, 'I'm Ted Deegan,' he'd have said, 'I'm Harley Bower, ma'am,' and probably she would have seen him around town, so she wouldn't have been afraid of him. Who would be afraid of Harley, anyway? And then I would have said, 'I'm sorry to be the bearer of bad news, but I think something has happened to your dog.' And I would have led her right around the side of the house at a fast clip before she could wonder how I'd found the dog *behind* the house, and I would have had the skull hidden in those shrubs, and as we passed I would have reached down and grabbed it and gone at her."

"God, Ted, you're diabolical," said Chief Henderson in amazement.

"It's only make-believe," Ted assured him earnestly.

"And then you would have turned out the lights," Sergeant Putnam interjected, "because she was lying in a pool of light."

"That's right," said Ted. "Anybody coming up the driveway could have seen her. And the neighbors might have thought it strange if the lights were on all night. Then I would have gone back to the woods and gotten the dog and brought him up there and made sure he got blood on his muzzle."

"My goodness." Bea shuddered. "I always thought of Harley as somewhat fastidious."

"Tell me," said Chief Henderson, "is there any reason why Albert couldn't have followed the same script?"

"Seems too well thought out for Albert."

"Oh, hell, I don't know," Chief Henderson declared in frustration, "but I sure am going to keep an eye on that boy. On Vesta, too, dammit. The whole family may be loaded with 'tendencies.'"

"You can get him on poaching charges, Chief."

"Right. And cause a wave of sympathy for poor, persecuted Albert."

"Well, at least one mystery is solved," Bea declared. "There seems to be no doubt about the cause of Lucy Mae's demise. Vesta talked to us a little more about it on the way home. Lucy Mae's head was crushed like an eggshell. Grandpa had a terrible temper."

"So Orianna's version of Lucy Mae's death was strictly fictional," mused Sergeant Putnam. "Yet it was her description that led me to think of the skull. In a way, you could say she solved her own murder."

"My, aren't we getting fanciful," murmured Chief Henderson, but Bea waved away his disparagement impatiently.

"I think it very fitting," she said, "in our tricentennial year, to have cleared away some of the murk from the past. We'll leave Orianna's death to the quadricentennial celebrants. That's only fair, don't you think?"